| DATE DUE | | |
|---|---|---|
| JUL 29 2006 | JUN 2006 | |
| OCT 04 2008 | JAN 0 6 2013 | |
| JAN 2 0 2009 | | |
| | | |
| | | |
| | | |
| | | |

# The Mysterious Mummer

# The Mysterious Mummer

L.M. Falcone

Kids Can Press

*10-03*
*17.00*

Kids Can Press acknowledges the financial support of the Ontario Arts Council,
the Canada Council for the Arts and the Government of Canada, through the
BPIDP, for our publishing activity.

Published in Canada by
Kids Can Press Ltd.
29 Birch Avenue
Toronto, ON M4V 1E2

Published in the U.S. by
Kids Can Press Ltd
2250 Military Road
Tonawanda, NY 14150

www.kidscanpress.com

Edited by Charis Wahl
Cover and interior designed by Marie Bartholomew
Interior graphics by Kathleen Collett

Printed and bound in Canada by Transcontinental Printing

CM 03 0 9 8 7 6 5 4 3 2 1
CM PA 03 0 9 8 7 6 5 4 3 2 1

**National Library of Canada Cataloguing in Publication Data**

Falcone, L. M. (Lucy M.), 1951–
        The mysterious mummer / L.M. Falcone.

ISBN 1-55337-376-6 (bound).    ISBN 1-55337-377-4 (pbk.)

I. Title.

PS8561.A574M98 2003          jC813'.6          C2002-905570-9

Kids Can Press is a **ℓΘΓⳑs**™ Entertainment company

TO TERRY KENNEDY,
WHOSE FAITH IN ME NEVER WAVERED

AND TO THE DIVINE SPIRIT THAT MOVES
IN ME IN SUCH WONDEROUS WAYS

"Promise you'll take me with you next time."

"I promise."

"Cross your heart and hope to die?"

"Cross my heart and hope to die."

Christmas holidays! No school, no homework! And what better place to celebrate than at Captain Cluck's Fabulous Fingers and Fries. Mom and I circled around to the drive-through and ordered. When we pulled back onto the street, I reached into my bag and grabbed the fattest fry I could find. As I opened my mouth wide — BAM! A van rear-ended us. We went flying through the intersection, jumped the curb, knocked down a mailbox, spun around four times and hit a tree. I didn't get a scratch. But my lunch was totaled. So was the car. Oh, and Mom broke her leg, in three places.

"You can't really want to spend your Christmas holidays in a hospital room?"

"I don't mind," I said, staring at the TV.

Mom shifted around on the bed to find a more comfortable position. Her leg was in a cast and the cast was in a sling raised practically over her head.

"It won't be much fun," she said.

I surfed with the remote.

"I'll have lots of fun with my friends."

"Paul's on a cruise and Danny has the flu."

Her leg might have been broken, but there was nothing wrong with her memory. My best friend, Paul Douglas, had promised me — no way was he going on any silly cruise, his parents couldn't make him. Well, they made him. And my other best friend, Danny Loader, got sick on the first day of Christmas break. Danny's useless when he's sick. Just lies in bed moaning. Doesn't even want to watch TV. Me? I can't live without it. Even commercials are great.

"This is Aunt Corinne's last Christmas in Monk's Cove, Joey," said my mom. "It'll be a good chance to spend some time there with her."

My eyes stayed glued to the set. "Where's she moving to?"

"She's not really sure. Someplace with more sunshine. She hasn't been herself since ... the tragedy, and the dreary weather in Monk's Cove doesn't help."

Mom leaned back and looked out the window. She had that faraway look in her eyes. I could tell she was feeling bad about her sister. My mom's one of those people who, when *you* get hurt, *she* feels the pain. Go figure.

Without even asking me, she had decided that since she'd be in the hospital over Christmas, the best place for me was at Aunt Corinne's. I doubt that Aunt Corinne thought it was such a great idea. Ever since Uncle Stephen died, she hadn't wanted much company. She wouldn't even let us go to the funeral.

"I've asked Mrs. Jerome next door to pack your suitcase." Mom was back in the game. She was persistent, I'll give her that. But so am I.

"I can't go and leave you here *alone* at *Christmas.*"

"I'll survive."

"Come Christmas morning you'll be bawling your eyes out from missing me so bad."

Mom smiled. "Of course I'll miss you, sweetheart. But with me here, there's no one to look after you."

"I'm thirteen, for crying out loud. That's old enough to look after myself."

"Aren't you the one who let that salesman into the house when I was out shopping?"

"He was working his way through college!"

"Selling knives?"

I put one hand over my heart, the other in the air. "I swear, I won't open the door to anybody holding a sharp object."

Mom changed tactics. "Your aunt's been feeling awfully lonely since Uncle Stephen died. Christmas is going to be tough for her. Having you around will brighten her holidays a little. Pretend you're a knight in shining armor on a mission of mercy."

"I'm sorry Aunt Corinne's lonely, but I *don't* want to go."

"Why *not?*" She was definitely getting frustrated. "I *know* you love your aunt and she's crazy about you. Why won't you go?!"

"Because!"

"Because *what?*"

"You *really* want to know?"

"Of course I want to know!"

"Okay. I won't go because Aunt Corinne doesn't have a television. *That's* why! Living without a television is just plain stupid. I'm not going. That's it. The end!"

There wasn't much of a view from the plane's window, and the bald guy sitting next to me snored. Normally this would drive me crazy, but there was a movie screen at the front, and since this was going to be the last time I could watch anything for a whole week, I plugged in my earphones and pumped up the volume.

The movie about beavers was okay but then they got to the good stuff — episodes of Mr. Bean! I laughed so hard ginger ale came shooting out my nose. The guy across the aisle must have got sprayed because he gave me a dirty look. What? Like I did it on purpose?

The thing I like about traveling alone is you get lots of attention. A flight attendant named Maureen slipped me five bags of peanuts and all the pop I could drink. Lucky she hadn't seen it shoot out my nose or she might have cut me off.

Somewhere during the third Mr. Bean, I got a funny feeling in my chest. A bit of excitement was starting to kick in. This wasn't good. When I get forced into doing something, I refuse to enjoy it. Once when my dad was still living with us, he dragged me to a father-son barbecue. I went on strike and refused to eat — no hamburgers, no hot dogs, no potato salad. Not even dessert. Then I sat out the Frisbee, volleyball and soccer games. It embarrassed my dad big time but he had it coming. You shouldn't make somebody go places they don't want to go, even if they're a kid. I didn't want to go to my aunt's for Christmas, I didn't want to be a knight in shining armor, and, most of all, I didn't want to go a whole week without television. So I squashed my excitement like a bug. When Aunt Corinne met me, I'd give her my sour look and she'd tell Mom, and that way Mom would learn that you can fly a kid to Newfoundland, but you can't make him like it.

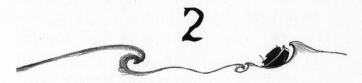

# 2

Maureen walked me off the plane and into the terminal. "My Aunt Corinne's really pretty," I told her. "She has blond hair and blue eyes. She's real easy to spot in a crowd."

Well, there wasn't much of a crowd and my aunt wasn't there.

"Maybe she's running a little late," Maureen said.

Suddenly I spotted an older man with thick hair and bushy eyebrows. He was holding up a sign that said "Welcome, Joey McDermet." Something about him looked familiar. Then I remembered. "That's Harry!"

The last time my mom and I came for a visit, Harry drove Aunt Corinne to the airport to pick us up. My aunt doesn't own a car. She never even learned to drive.

"Let's check it out," said Maureen, walking me over to Harry.

"Hi, Harry."

Harry shook my hand. "Well, hello, Joey! Welcome back to Newfoundland."

Harry shook Maureen's hand, too. "I'm Harry Walsh, a friend of Joey's aunt."

Maureen smiled. "I was told Mrs. Simmonds would be meeting Joey today."

"I know, I know," said Harry. "But she didn't feel well, so she sent the next best thing ... *me!*"

Maureen wasn't about to just hand me over. She made us wait while she talked with her supervisor, and then they called Aunt Corinne. When everything checked out, off we went.

Outside, the cold Newfoundland air hit me like a brick. "My van's right over there," Harry said, pointing. "Parked real close so we wouldn't freeze our butts off. Weather's been crappy."

The van was bright red. Harry lifted my suitcase and said, "Hop in before you freeze your tush."

Harry was the unofficial free taxi service of Monk's Cove. If anybody needed a ride to go grocery shopping or for a hospital visit or anything, they called him.

As soon as I opened the door, I noticed a television set propped up against the back seat. It made me grumpy all over again. When Harry got in, he saw me looking at the TV. "Your aunt asked if she could borrow one of my TVs while you're visitin'."

"You're kidding! It's for *me?!*"

"Sure is."

"Aunt Corinne's *never* had a television. Said she never would."

"Guess she's changed 'er mind."

"All right!"

As we drove along, I remembered my aunt's boring lectures about television turning my brain to mush. "It'll drain the life right out of you," she'd say. "If you want to be an interesting person, *unplug* the TV." She must have said it a hundred times. Did I listen? Not on your life. I'm plenty interesting already.

I liked Harry. It felt like I'd known him forever. Some people are like that. You just feel comfortable right away. He handed me a small card and said, "That's my phone number. You ever need a ride, just give me a call."

"Thanks." I tucked the card into my coat pocket, but I knew I wouldn't be calling him. Now that I had a TV, I wasn't planning on going out much.

About half an hour later we arrived at the ferry that takes people over to Monk's Cove. We made it just in time. The bars were already coming down, but Harry sped up and honked the horn. Then he put his hands together like he was praying. The bar went up again and we drove aboard. There was barely enough room for us.

"Lucky break," said Harry. "We'd've had to wait a couple of hours if they hadn't let us on."

Harry turned off the engine but left the key in the ignition. We got out and walked up some iron stairs to the deck. The ferry was pretty crowded but there was a bit of space on a wooden bench next to a man and three boys. Harry offered me the spot and said, "I need to take a leak."

I squeezed in next to the smallest boy. He lifted his mittened hand and said, "Hi." I said hi back and tried not to look at the stream of snot running down to his mouth. He grinned, stuck out his tongue and *licked* it. Like it was ice cream or something. I turned and stared out over the railing.

An icy wind blew as the ferry headed to Monk's Cove. I'd never felt cold like this before. It actually hurt. Up ahead, the clouds looked really dark, and people started pointing at them. The sky got darker and darker and waves slapped against the hull. The man sitting on the bench with me said, "Looks like a storm's headin' this way." His boys moved in closer to him. I wished I could, too. I must have looked worried because he said, "Just sit tight. It'll blow over real quick."

A flash of lightning streaked across the gray sky, followed by the loudest crack of thunder I'd ever heard. Then rain came from out of nowhere. One of the passengers made the sign of the cross and a kid started crying. Suddenly, the ferry lurched and two men lost their balance. The little boy with the runny nose whimpered and buried his face in his brother's shoulder. "It's okay, Kenny," said his brother. "Like Dad said, it'll pass quick." Kenny didn't believe him. Neither did I. But right then, the wind suddenly stopped, like someone had turned it off. The rain eased up and the sky got lighter. Somebody laughed and, just like that, everybody felt better.

Harry finally came back. "Guess what I was doin' when the ferry lurched? Good thing I was sittin' down."

Twenty minutes later a horn blasted and the ferry docked in Monk's Cove. Since we were the last to get on, we were first off.

As we drove along, Harry talked about a Christmas play that the youth group was putting on and about all the baking his wife was doing. "I have to let out my pants every Christmas," he said with a laugh. Then Harry suddenly got serious. "Joey? Remember at the airport when I said your aunt wasn't feeling up to traveling today?"

"Yeah."

"Well ..." He took a deep breath. "It's not just today."

I frowned. "Is Aunt Corinne sick?"

Harry nodded. "She's been under the weather for a couple of weeks now. A real bad flu went around and she just can't shake it. It's this darn cold. We've had some pretty bad winters before, but this year, I tell ya ..." He shook his head. "Never seen nothin' like it. You make sure you button up real good when you go out."

"Don't worry about me, Harry. I'm planning on staying *inside* — with the TV."

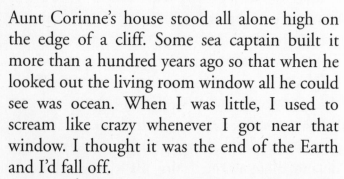

Aunt Corinne's house stood all alone high on the edge of a cliff. Some sea captain built it more than a hundred years ago so that when he looked out the living room window all he could see was ocean. When I was little, I used to scream like crazy whenever I got near that window. I thought it was the end of the Earth and I'd fall off.

On one side of the roof was a widow's walk. That's a wooden platform with rails around it. Sailors' wives used to look out over the water, waiting for their husbands to come home. I guess it's called a widow's walk because so many sailors didn't come back. Just like Uncle Stephen.

Harry pulled up beside the house and stopped the van.

"Joey?"

"Yeah?"

Harry spoke really slowly. "You know your aunt's been under the weather for a couple of weeks now."

"Uh-huh." He'd already told me that.

"Well, she's ... not her usual self."

"I understand," I said as I opened the door and jumped out.

"Joey?"

I turned back. Harry had a strange look on his face.

"If you need anything, *anything* at all, just call me. Promise?"

"Okay."

I slammed the door. Harry got out and handed me my suitcase. I grabbed the handle and dragged it around to the back and up the wooden steps to the little porch off the kitchen. Stamping my feet to get the snow off, I dropped the suitcase and shouted, "Aunt Corinne, I'm here!"

No answer. I slipped off my boots and stepped into the kitchen. Oh man! Dirty dishes were all over the table, piled in the sink, everywhere. And the garbage was overflowing. Aunt Corinne must really be sick to leave a mess like this.

"Aunt Corinne!" I shouted again.

The door to the living room slowly opened. What I saw made my jaw drop.

# 3

My beautiful aunt looked like an old lady. Her face was gray and her shoulders were stooped. Her hair was greasy and stringy, like it hadn't been washed for a long time.

"Aunt Corinne?"

Harry came in carrying the television set. I heard a low voice say, "Just put it in the bedroom beside the bathroom." It didn't sound anything like my aunt. Her voice had always been sweet and friendly.

Harry went past her through to the living room. That left me alone with this ... person.

"Um, Harry told me you weren't feeling well," I said. What I really felt like saying was, "You look *really* bad."

"I'm fine. Just a little tired. Haven't been sleeping well lately."

If you asked me, she looked like she hadn't slept for a month.

I couldn't think of anything else to say. What was taking Harry so long? I finally came up with, "Um, thanks for getting the TV for me."

"There isn't much to do around here," said my aunt. "The weather's miserable." She slowly eased herself into a chair and stared at the salt and pepper shakers. "You might as well watch. It doesn't matter."

What? Aunt Corinne not caring if I watched TV? Who was this woman?

Finally, Harry came back. "It's plugged in and ready to go. You'll only get a few stations but they're not half bad."

"Thanks," I muttered.

Harry turned to my aunt. "Is there anythin' in town you need, Corinne? Groceries or —"

Aunt Corinne cut him off. "I'm fine, Harry."

"Well then, I'd best be headin' out." Harry pulled on his gloves. "Lois Clancy needs a lift to choir practice." He turned to me. "You know, we miss yer aunt's lovely voice." He gave Aunt Corinne a smile. "She sings like an angel."

The compliment didn't work. Aunt Corinne just kept staring at the salt and pepper. Then Harry was gone. I wanted to race after him and beg him not to leave me here. But I didn't. I just stood there. Finally, Aunt Corinne pushed herself up from the table.

"I'm feeling a little tired," she said. "I think I'll go lie down." She shuffled to the door.

"There's food in the fridge, and you've got the TV and plenty of books." With that, she pushed through the swinging door and disappeared. That's when I lunged for the phone on the wall. I had memorized the hospital number because Mom would be there the whole time I was away. The switchboard took forever to answer.

"Valley Glen Hospital."

"Could I have room 304 please?"

Two rings and Mom picked up. "Hello."

"I don't like it here." I said it hard and serious. "I wanna come home."

"I see you made it safe and sound."

"*Listen* to me. Something really strange is going on."

"How's Aunt Corinne? I'll bet seeing you cheered her up."

"Did you hear what I said?!" I was shouting now. "Something really *strange* is going on here!" I glanced at the door, worried my aunt might have heard.

"Like what?"

"Like Aunt Corinne," I whispered. "She's changed. *Really* changed."

"She's probably a little sad, what with Christmas right around the corner. That's why you're there. To brighten things up."

"Fat chance. It's like a morgue in here! And Aunt Corinne's the corpse! I'm not kidding, Mom. She's scary."

"Now stop exaggerating. With you around, she'll feel better and then she'll look better, too. Trust me."

"But, Mom —"

"Put her on, Joey. I want to say hello."

"She's lying down," I said. "She's not feeling well."

"Then don't bother her. We'll talk later. You have a good time, okay, sweetheart?"

"Mom!"

"Bye, Joey."

It was no use. She wasn't buying it. As I hung up the phone, I thought I heard a scratching sound under the sink. I stood still and listened really carefully. Nothing. I pulled open the cupboard door. Inside was another garbage bin full right to the top, some cleaning things and a few sponges. I poked my head in and listened but didn't hear anything, so I just pushed the door shut.

After I hung my coat on a hook by the back door, I dragged my suitcase to the bedroom I always stay in. It looked the same — a big comfortable bed with an Amish quilt, a nightstand and a dresser with a mirror. Through the window I could see the rocky hill leading down to the town. The only thing that was different was the TV. Harry had set it up on a stand next to the closet. There was no remote but I could live with that.

I flipped through some snowy stations till I landed on a channel that came in clear. *The 5,000 Fingers of Dr. T* was on. I've seen that movie a million times, but watching TV is so — I don't know — it's like a kid's favorite blanket. It just feels good. What can I say?

About an hour later, my stomach growled. When the next commercial came on, I ran down the hall, through the living room and into the kitchen. Whipping open the fridge door, I was shocked to see empty shelves. Well, almost empty. There was some brown lettuce, two shriveled apples and a bowl of dried-up spaghetti. That was it.

I checked the cupboards and found a jar of jam and a box of crackers. The box was so light I thought it was empty. I was really happy to see five crackers sitting at the bottom. I got a knife and a plate, spread out the crackers and loaded on the jam, really thick. Then I crunched up the box and flung it toward the garbage. It bounced off the wall and landed on the floor behind the bin. I thought of leaving it there — who'd notice? But I felt guilty, so I reached behind to get it.

Snap!

A mousetrap was squeezing my fingertips! I let out a really loud scream, grabbed the metal bar with my left hand and pried it off. It snapped again as it hit the wood. The pain was horrible.

"Aunt Corinne!"

The kitchen door swung open. "What are you screaming for?" Aunt Corinne demanded.

"My fingers! They got caught in the mousetrap! It really hurts. Do something!"

She grabbed my hand and stuck it under the cold water tap.

"It *hurts*."

"Stop acting like a baby!"

I couldn't believe she'd said that. She turned off the water and looked at the welt that had come up. "You'll live."

My fingers throbbed like crazy but I just clenched my teeth and stomped out of the kitchen. When I got to my bedroom, I slammed the door as hard as I could. Then I kicked it. How could she treat me like this? Why did she hate me? I sat down hard on the bed. I'd stay locked in my room for the rest of the week. That'd show her.

I held my fingers as tightly as I could to stop the pain. I couldn't concentrate on the movie but I kept the TV on for company. Finally, I fell asleep.

When I woke up I looked over at the clock. It was three o'clock. As I sat up, my stomach growled again. It wanted to be fed. If I didn't eat soon, I'd get really cranky — and I was on my way to cranky already. I opened the door, scouted the hall, and saw that Aunt Corinne's bedroom door was closed. I headed to the kitchen for those crackers. When I got to the counter, they were gone. Aunt Corinne had thrown them into the garbage.

Fine. If she didn't want to feed me, I'd buy my own darn food. I marched over to my coat and checked my wallet. There was a twenty-dollar bill, a ten and a five. Good. I pulled on my coat and headed to town.

Walking down the hill and along the road, I felt really alone. I wished my mom had come with me. I wished anybody had come with me.

I remembered the last time my family was here for Christmas. Dad was still with us, so I must have been nine or ten. Aunt Corinne went all out, decorating her house and buying the biggest tree she could find. She baked for weeks before the holidays and I ate tons of cookies. I missed that Aunt Corinne. Thinking about her made me feel even lonelier.

The wind was blowing pretty hard and I could hear the ocean waves crashing against the rocks. Then, out of nowhere, a plastic bag flew by. It kept filling with air and blowing along, landing for a second, then up it went again. It kept me company.

After about ten minutes, my teeth were chattering and my forehead felt like a knife was stabbing it. Then my nose started running. I searched my pockets for a tissue but came up empty, so I used the back of my hand. In about half a minute, my fingers stung so bad I tucked them deep inside my pocket. Putting my head down against the wind, I kept walking.

By the time I finally arrived, I was dead tired and starving to death. When I looked up, I saw that the whole town was ready for Christmas. Big gold bells with red ribbons were strung across the road and twinkling lights had been wound around the trees. Everything looked magical. As I walked along, I forgot about how mean and ugly my aunt was.

A horn honked loudly, making me jump. It was Harry pulling up in front of the antique shop. "How's it goin', Joey?" he called out.

"Fine." A lie. A big fat lie.

"Ya didn't walk all the way from the house, did ya?"

I nodded.

"In *this* weather?"

I nodded again.

"Why didn't you call me?"

I shrugged.

"You still have my number, don't you?"

I nodded again. Even though my hands were practically numb, I could still feel his card in my pocket.

"Don't you be afraid to phone, okay?"

Just as Harry reached the shop door, words finally came. "Harry?" He stopped and turned around. "I think my brain's frozen."

Harry walked over, put his big arm around my shoulder and said, "Come on. Let's go get us some hot chocolate."

We walked across the street to the coffee shop. A lady was just coming out. "Merry Christmas, Harry," she said cheerily.

"Merry Christmas, Jan."

As soon as we stepped inside, the warm air poured over me. It felt so good. Then my body started shaking.

"That's my favorite spot," said Harry, indicating a table by the window. "Why don't you go and sit down and I'll order for us."

I managed to walk over to the table and plunk myself down. With the warmth of the room, my ears began to burn. Frostbite for sure. I pictured my ears turning black and some doctor chopping them off. I read somewhere that actually happened to some kid.

"... I seen 'er walkin' — back and forth, back and forth." A man with a gravelly voice was sitting a couple of tables away. "Gone cracked, she 'as."

"Loneliness, is what it is," said a short, plump lady with dark hair. "Loneliness can do that. Make ya wander around with no port to call home."

"But 'ave ya *seen* 'er? Looks like a corpse, she does."

These people had to be talking about my aunt. I listened more closely. The dark-haired lady stirred her coffee and shook her head. "She's not eatin', that's why. Cora and I brung over a stew and fresh-baked bread. Wouldn't even open the door."

"Did the same when Reverend Joseph dropped by," said another lady.

Just then Harry came back holding a tray with two steaming mugs and two doughnuts. He sat down and slid one of the hot chocolates across the table. "There you go, Joey. That should warm you up a bit."

I wrapped my hands around the mug for the warmth and took a sip. Best hot chocolate I ever tasted. I eyeballed the two doughnuts.

"Honey-glazed or raspberry?" Harry asked.

"Both." I couldn't believe I'd said that. "I — I mean — they're both my favorite. But today I feel more like raspberry."

Harry passed over the powdered raspberry doughnut. I practically swallowed it whole. Harry's eyes widened. "Isn't yer aunt feedin' you?" he laughed.

"Oh, sure. Lots of food. Tons. It's just ... I really like doughnuts."

That seemed to satisfy him. What went on at home was nobody's business. Mom pounded that into my head after Dad left.

"Has Aunt Corinne really gone cracked?" One minute I was telling myself to keep quiet and the next I was blurting out the question.

"Who's been fillin' yer head with such nonsense?"

"Those people were talking," I whispered. "Over there." I jabbed my finger toward the other table.

Harry glanced over and shook his head. "That's just old Pete. He and his friends like to have a good chin wag 'round this time of day. Don't pay them no mind."

"My aunt," I said slowly. "She isn't ... like she used to be."

Harry nodded. "I know." Then he took a sip of his hot chocolate. "The light's gone out of her again."

"Again?"

Harry put his cup down. "After your Uncle Stephen died, your aunt was really broken up. Anybody would be, o' course. But after a time she started healin'. Now, with Christmas comin' and their anniversary right after ..."

I'd forgotten about the anniversary. Aunt Corinne and Uncle Stephen got married the day after Christmas. It's called St. Stephen's day. I thought that was funny, his name being Stephen and all.

"It's her first Christmas without 'im," Harry went on. "The first one's always the worst." He looked out the window. "I lost my son some years back. That first Christmas pretty near killed me. Maxine, that's the wife, she couldn't talk for a whole month before and cried for a whole month after."

"Gee, I'm sorry, Harry."

Harry gave me a little smile and then leaned forward. "Once Christmas is over and the anniversary passes, I believe she'll start to feel better. Be patient."

Maybe he was right. Or maybe this is how people with a broken heart died. A minute at a time. Getting sadder and sadder.

Wait a second — Aunt Corinne wasn't sad. She was mean. When you're sad you don't ignore people and you don't yell at them for no reason and you don't tell them to stop acting like a baby when they get hurt. I really wanted to tell Harry what Aunt Corinne had done but I couldn't — it felt like tattling. At school once, I saw some kids throwing stones at a teacher's car. When I told the principal, they got in trouble — their parents even got called. Somehow the kids found out I was the one who told on them, so they waited for me after school and beat me up. I just took it — figured they'd hit me even harder if I fought back — but I wish I could have got in just one good punch. Since then I've never ratted on anybody and I wasn't going to now.

Harry and I finished our doughnuts and hot chocolate, then he said he had to pick up Maxine at the hairdresser's. "Want a lift home?"

"No thank you."

He put his hand on my shoulder. "You just call if you need anything. Okay?"

"Okay."

From the coffee shop, I headed straight for the grocery store.

It was pretty small and there wasn't great stuff or anything, but I picked up two loaves of bread, a jar of peanut butter, some Cheez Whiz, a carton of milk and a couple bags of salt and vinegar chips. When I got to the cashier, she said, "Joey, isn't it?"

I nodded. "Yes. Hi." I had no idea who she was.

"Last time you were in here you bought up *all* my saltwater taffy!" Now I remembered. It was the best taffy ever. Couldn't get enough. "Is yer dear aunt feelin' any better?"

I nodded. "A little."

"Give 'er me regards, will ya? Tell 'er Edna at the store is keepin' 'er in me prayers."

"I'll tell her."

As I stepped out the door, I realized my ears still hurt, so I stopped at a used clothing store. There was a shelf full of hats — all stupid-looking, with flaps that hung over your ears. Did I care? No way. I wanted those flaps, bad.

I waited till I was outside to put on the hat. I took it out of the bag and tried to pull the darn price tag off. Finally I gave up and just plunked the hat on my head and let the tag dangle. I must have looked like a real geek, so I kept my head down till I got to the edge of town. From there I didn't have to worry about being seen. Nobody in their right mind was out walking today. Nobody but me.

# 4

Back at the house, I took my boots off but kept my coat on. The cold had seeped right inside my bones. I slid the grocery bag onto the counter and lifted out the bread and peanut butter. Unscrewing the lid, I stuck my nose practically inside and breathed deeply. Then I pulled six slices out of the bread bag. They were extra thick, the way I like them. I scooped up as much peanut butter as the knife could hold and slathered it over the bread. Then I paired up the slices and smooshed them down. After pouring myself a glass of milk, I headed for my room.

I could hear music coming from down the hall. It sounded really pretty. I stopped and listened, thinking maybe Aunt Corinne was feeling better. She always liked music — said that people should talk less and listen to music more.

As I stood there an idea hit me — offer her some food. I walked down to her room and knocked. No answer. Maybe she'd fallen asleep. I'd try again later. Just then her door creaked open. Aunt Corinne stood behind it, looking out through the small opening. I could only see half her face.

"What do you want?" she asked in a sleepy voice.

"Sorry. I didn't mean to wake you," I said. "I just thought maybe you wanted something to eat." I held the plate up so she could see the sandwiches, hoping she'd say yes and maybe let me in. I'd been in her house for almost a whole day and we hadn't even talked yet.

My aunt stared at the plate and finally said, "I'm not hungry." She started to close the door.

"Do you want to watch TV with me?" Dumb question.

"Maybe later," she said in a low voice. "I have a headache." The door closed.

As I walked away, I heard the click of a lock. Why would she lock herself in her bedroom? Then it hit me. She wasn't locking herself *in,* she was locking me *out.* Why? What was she hiding in there? What didn't she want me to see?

I went to my room, turned on the TV and, leaning against the headboard, made myself comfortable. I gulped down the first sandwich. Nothing ever tasted so good.

*Gilligan's Island* was on. I love that show but

I couldn't concentrate. As I finished off the second sandwich, my curiosity got the better of me. I swung my legs over the side of the bed and left the room. Sliding into my boots I went out the door, down the steps and around the side of the house, the side closest to the edge of the cliff.

Aunt Corinne's bedroom was the second window down. I tiptoed over to it and stretched up to peek inside. The curtains were drawn but there was a tiny space along the edge. If I held my head just right, I could see in. But all I could see was Aunt Corinne's bed, and she wasn't in it. Something strange was going on in that room. I could feel it in my bones. But what could I do? Force her to let me in? It wouldn't work. She'd just get mad again.

I headed back to my room. A cooking show with a really fat chef was on. I flipped through the few stations that came in clearly and found a movie that was just starting called *It's a Wonderful Life*. I don't like black and white films very much but I thought, What the heck? At least somebody was having a good time.

I still didn't take my coat off because the place was freezing. Crawling under the covers, I reached for the last sandwich and watched George Bailey, the guy in the film, give up doing the things he really wanted to do so that other people would be happy. Finally, he got so depressed he wanted to die. It wasn't such a wonderful life after all.

I fell asleep watching the movie, don't know for how long, but when I woke up, I was really thirsty. I kicked off the blankets and got up. Just as I reached for the doorknob, I heard Aunt Corinne's door open, then close. She was finally coming out of her room. I heard the floor creak as she walked past. I couldn't decide if I should go talk to her, but then I figured she'd had plenty of time alone. Maybe she wouldn't mind.

I stepped into the hall. When I got to the living room, I heard the back door close. I looked over at the clock on the mantel. It was 11:35. Why was she going out this late? I ran into the kitchen and looked out the window. There she was, holding a lantern, heading down the hill. I jumped into my boots and bolted out the door. I could see the light from the lantern and figured Aunt Corinne took it so she could see where she was going. There weren't any streetlights or anything like that in Monk's Cove.

"Aunt Corinne! Wait up!" I raced down the hill after her. The light stopped moving. As I got closer, she spun around. Her eyes blazed.

"Why are you following me?!"

"I — I just wondered where you were going, that's all. It's so late."

She held the lantern up higher. The light and shadows made her face look evil. "What business is it of yours? I have a right to go anywhere I please!"

I couldn't believe she was yelling at me like that. "I'm sorry," I finally squeaked out.

"How dare you sneak around after me!" Spit flew out of her mouth. "Go home! Just go home! And mind your own business!"

I turned and ran back up the hill, tears streaming down my face. I hadn't done anything wrong! Why was she so mad at me? I raced up the steps, flung open the door and stormed inside. The next thing I knew, my fist was hitting the wall. I pounded and pounded. And then screamed. I hated my aunt more than I'd ever hated anyone in my whole life.

Suddenly, the lights went out.

The darkness startled me so much I shut up. "Aunt Corinne?"

There was no answer. I couldn't see a thing so I just stood still, listening in the eerie silence. Finally, I reached out and patted around until my fingers found the light switch. I flicked it up and down a few times. Nothing.

As I stood there wondering what to do, I heard the roar of the ocean and the sound of crashing waves. I swear I heard voices too, lots of them, all talking together. Where were these people? What were they doing here? I listened harder. There they were again. Then they stopped. Each time the waves crashed, I heard the voices. I must be imagining things. It's just the sound of water. That's all.

How could anything be this dark? Maybe outside I'd be able to see better. I put my arms out, stepped down into the porch area and felt my way to the back door. I found the handle of the screen door and pushed. Something brushed up against me.

I screamed and rushed back into the house, tripping over the step to the kitchen. I felt a sharp pain as my knees and arms hit the floor. Then I tasted blood. I must have bitten the inside of my lip.

Scrambling up, I headed for the door to the living room. My leg banged against a chair. I touched it with my hand, then moved around it. I heard something behind me. The moon must have come out a bit because I could see a shadow at the window.

Something was in the house.

The shadow stared at me. I couldn't breathe. Sweat slid down my forehead as I moved sideways one step at a time, trying to get to the living room.

As the shadow moved toward me, I let out a yell. It worked — whatever it was moved back. I turned my head slowly to the right, following the moving shape. Then I heard something scuttle across the floor. The shadow let out a horrifying shriek and leaped. I screamed my lungs out till I realized the shadow hadn't leaped at me — it had gone straight to the floor and was tearing something apart. I freaked out.

As I grabbed for something to throw at it, my arm hit the kettle on the stove. It crashed to the floor. I heard another screech and saw the shadow tear out of the house. I raced to the back door, slammed it shut and locked it.

Through the porch window I saw the shadow bolt across the yard. It was a cat! A darn cat!

I caught my breath and tried to calm down. My eyes must have got used to the darkness because there was enough light now to make out some forms — the fridge, the table. My legs moved slowly through the kitchen and into the living room. They wouldn't stop shaking.

Things seemed darker in the living room. Hardly any light came through the window, but I knew there was a clear path from the kitchen across the living room to the hallway. Still, I kept my arms straight out in front of me, sliding my feet across the carpet like I was cross-country skiing. The floorboards creaked and my whole body tensed. How blind people can walk down streets I'll never know. I barely had to go fifteen steps and it seemed to be taking forever.

Once I got to the hall I noticed a golden light at the far end. It was coming from the crack under Aunt Corinne's bedroom door. That didn't make sense. How could the electricity be on just in her room?

As I got closer to her door, I noticed a strange smell. It was definitely coming from her room. What *was* it? I knew my aunt wouldn't like me going inside. The old Aunt Corinne wouldn't have minded a bit, but this new, mean one would probably go berserk. Then again, she'd left, going who knows where, so she'd never know. I turned the knob, slowly opened the door and went inside.

Candles burned everywhere, dozens of them, each one white with a golden flame. I stepped farther in. A table in the corner had a cloth draped over it. It looked like an altar with a wreath of flowers and two candles on top. In the center was a framed photograph of Uncle Stephen. He looked really happy.

When I got closer I saw that the flowers were black roses. They'd probably been red once but they had dried black. Beside the roses were three crystal angels. Propped up against the middle one was a card with words on it. I picked it up. "Incantation for the Dead." This was really bad. I'd seen enough movies to know that incantations were done by *witches*.

Out of the corner of my eye, I saw a figure reflected in the mirror. I gasped and spun around. A woman was standing right behind me! I yelled and jumped back, tripping over the stool in front of the altar. The woman didn't move.

Then I realized it wasn't a woman at all. It was a dressmaker's dummy. On it hung a wedding dress. It looked creepy just standing there, a body with no face and no hands. A veil was draped over the head. On the floor, around the bottom of the dress, were more dead roses. There was also a photograph — of Uncle Stephen and Aunt Corinne on their wedding day. The dress my aunt was wearing was the one on the dummy. In the picture, Aunt Corinne was holding a bouquet of red roses.

I got up and looked around a little more. The room was a shrine, to Uncle Stephen. Just like a shrine to a saint. Did Aunt Corinne pray to Uncle Stephen? As I slowly walked around the room, it hit me — Aunt Corinne really was crazy. I was living with a crazy person.

# 5

It was time to call my mom again. This time I'd make her listen. There was a phone beside Aunt Corinne's bed. I quickly walked over and picked it up. No dial tone. Electricity shouldn't affect the phone. I pushed the button a few times. Still nothing. Maybe it wasn't plugged in. Mom unplugs her bedroom phone when she wants to take a nap. Maybe Aunt Corinne did, too.

I felt around under the bed for the cord. My hand touched a book. I pulled it out and saw a bookmark about halfway through the pages. As I opened to that page, I knew something important would be on it. One line was highlighted in bright yellow. "And the sea gave up all the dead that were in it." The window rattled loudly.

I dropped the book and stared. It was just the wind.

Stay calm.

I bent to pick up the book and spotted the phone cord. I was right. It had been unplugged. I jammed it into the outlet and — yes! — a dial tone.

I punched the numbers and waited. "Come on, come on, pick up." No one did. How could a hospital not answer the phone? *Somebody* had to be there. But it just kept ringing. I slammed down the receiver.

Taking one of the candles, I made my way back to my room, went over to the closet and pulled open the door. Was it still there? Please be there. The candle didn't cast much light, so I carefully set it down and crawled into the dark closet. Feeling around, I found some boxes and lots of shoes. It had to be here somewhere. Finally, my fingers touched it. Gripping it tightly, I pulled it out — a baseball bat Aunt Corinne had bought for me. She always encouraged outdoor sports. Thank you, Aunt Corinne.

I carried the candle and the bat to the nightstand. Then I went to the door. No lock. Too bad. I dragged the armchair across the floor and put it so it faced the door. Then I sat down holding the bat. "Stay awake. Stay awake." I said it over and over.

Aunt Corinne would have to come back sooner or later, and you never know what a crazy person might do to you when you're sleeping. So I sat there, staring at the door.

I waited for over an hour — I know because I kept looking at my watch. "Stay awake. Stay awake." But I couldn't.

Suddenly, my body jerked. How long had I been sleeping? I checked my watch — 4:30 in the morning. Had Aunt Corinne come back?

I got a tight hold on the baseball bat and took the three steps to the door. Before I opened it, I tested the light switch. Still dead. I turned the doorknob as quietly as I could and poked my head out. I looked down the hall toward my aunt's room. Everything was dark.

Creak ... creak ... creak. What was that?!

The sound came from the other direction, from the living room. Someone — or something — was in the house. Was it Aunt Corinne? Creak ... creak ... creak. What could it be? I crept along the dark hallway. Creak ... creak ... creak.

What *was* it?

At the living room door, I raised the bat, ready to swing. Then I slowly leaned my head around the corner. Even though it was still pretty dark, I could make out a figure. Someone was sitting in the rocking chair going back and forth, back and forth. They were facing the window that overlooked the ocean. Creak ... creak ... creak ... Always the same rhythm. Creak ... creak ... creak ...

"Who's there?" I whispered.

The creaking stopped.

"What do you want?" The voice was dry and crackly but it was definitely Aunt Corinne's. I lowered the bat.

"I want to talk to you."

She started rocking again, still staring out the window.

"Aunt Corinne?"

Creak ... creak ... creak ... I walked up behind her. That's when I saw what she was staring at. A huge mass of water was silently receding. I watched, mesmerized, as the wave rose higher and higher and higher. Then it stopped and a couple of seconds later it started bearing down on us with unbelievable speed. The wall of black water got closer and closer and closer. Then, with the thunder of a thousand breakers, it hit!

6

I tried to get away from the water but I couldn't move. Couldn't stop screaming either. The door burst open and Aunt Corinne came rushing in. "What's wrong?" she shouted.

The screaming wouldn't stop.

She grabbed me and shook me. "You're having a nightmare. Wake up." She shook me even harder. "Wake up! Wake up!"

"I am awake!" I yelled. But she wouldn't stop. Didn't she hear me? "I *am* awake!"

Her eyes blazed and her lips snarled. A low growl came from deep inside her throat, then her mouth opened and a snake sprang out!

I jerked awake dripping in sweat, my heart thumping like mad. My breath came in loud rasps and I felt so scared my stomach ached. Was I really awake this time? Please, let me be awake.

I looked around. I was in the bedroom, still sitting in the armchair holding the baseball bat. It was just a nightmare. I kept telling myself that over and over. Just a nightmare. Then I realized — I had peed my pants.

Pulling my jeans and underwear down, I dried myself off. Then I tucked the wet clothes under the bed until I could wash them. I slipped into my pajamas and as dawn streamed through the window, I curled up in bed and tried not to cry. I wanted to be home more than anything I've ever wanted in my whole life. I was so tired. But I was afraid to fall asleep. What if another nightmare came? Some people say dreams are just pictures in your head. Well, they're wrong. I think we go somewhere in our dreams and what happens really does happen — only it's in another dimension or something. But it's still real.

I could hear my watch ticking, and the sound comforted me. I tried not to think of anything. Nothing at all. I fell asleep. Deeply, soundly asleep.

The hum of a car engine filtered through the window. My eyes slowly opened — daylight. What time was it? I looked at my watch — One thirty in the afternoon! I've never slept that late. I got out of bed, crossed the room and looked through the frost-covered window. I could just see the words "Prescott Real Estate" on the side of a station wagon. The driver's door opened and out stepped a little man in a dark blue overcoat holding a large envelope. He disappeared around the back of the house and then I heard a knock.

While I waited for Aunt Corinne to answer, there was another knock, louder this time. I listened at my bedroom door but couldn't hear anything, so I poked my head out. Sounds came from the living room. I stepped into the hallway and walked along it as quietly as I could. When I got to the living room I saw my aunt lighting some logs in the fireplace. She didn't see me watching her. When the third knock came she stood up and reset the clock on the mantel. I really wanted to ask why she wasn't answering, but I didn't want to give her any excuse to get mad at me again, so I kept my mouth shut. Finally, she turned and walked through to the kitchen. I heard the back door open and my aunt say, "Mr. Elsworth. Come in."

"There's something I want to show you, Mrs. Simmonds. Could you come outside?"

It felt strange hearing my aunt called Mrs. Simmonds — she'd only married my Uncle Stephen a year ago. I opened the kitchen door a crack and watched my aunt pull her coat on over her bathrobe. Then she stepped out the door, still wearing her slippers. I moved into the kitchen and hopped onto the counter by the window. Even though fog surrounded the house, I could see my aunt and Mr. Elsworth beside some high bushes. The bushes had burlap sacks over them, tied in two places with rope. They looked like small, fat monks in robes with no faces and pointy hoods.

Mr. Elsworth was saying he had a copy of the inspection report and it wasn't good. Then he bent down. When I craned my neck, I could just see him crouched low, pointing under the house. I couldn't make out what he was saying, but when he stood up again, I caught his final words, "... the foundation isn't safe."

"What you're saying is I won't get much for the house." Aunt Corinne's voice was really tight.

"I have to be honest with you, Mrs. Simmonds. I don't think you'll find a buyer ... This house is a death trap."

Aunt Corinne wrapped her arms around herself and didn't say anything.

"I'm sorry," said Mr. Elsworth. "I know you were counting on selling, but you can still get something for the land."

"Is it dangerous to stay in the house?" she asked. "My nephew's visiting."

"Not for now." Mr. Elsworth shook his head. "I wouldn't stay into spring, though. Rain's gonna be the problem. I can send someone over to shore up the beams if it'll make you feel —"

My aunt didn't let him finish. "Thanks for coming by, Mr. Elsworth." She turned and walked away.

Mr. Elsworth stood there for a bit. Then he shuffled the papers back into the envelope, got into his car and drove away.

I waited a really long time but my aunt didn't come inside. Where had she gone? It was freezing out. I jumped down from the counter and opened the back door. Aunt Corinne was standing at the edge of the cliff, staring out over the ocean, like she was waiting for someone. It didn't take a genius to figure out who. But the dead don't come back — at least they better not.

I closed the door and leaned against it, thinking about my Uncle Stephen. I didn't know very much about him. Mom told me he had moved away from the island a long time ago to find work, but came home for his father's funeral. Aunt Corinne met up with him and they fell madly in love. Got married three months later. A whirlwind romance, Mom called it. The two of them just went off to the local minister the day after Christmas and said "I do." The only other person at the wedding was Stephen's mother. She lives in the next village, so they couldn't very well *not* invite her. Mothers are sensitive about things like that.

THUMP! I spun around. What was that? THUMP! The sound came from outside. THUMP! I opened the wooden door. A huge gray cat with a flat face and one ear missing was trying to get inside, hurling itself hard against the screen door.

"Get away from here!" Aunt Corinne's voice startled me. "Go on! Get away!"

The cat ran off. My aunt stepped inside and shut the door. "That's a *vicious* cat, Joey. Don't *ever* let it inside." Then, in a softer voice she said, "Okay, honey?"

Honey? Had she just called me honey?

"Sure," I said, moving out of her way. Her cheeks were red from the cold. The color made her look better.

"It kills squirrels, birds — anything it can get its hands on."

Cats don't have hands, I thought. But I kept the thought to myself.

"The weather's so bad it has nothing to eat, but I refuse to feed it. Tried once. Felt sorry for it." She moved over to the sink, lifted the kettle, filled it with water and placed it on the stove. "Darn thing bit me. Tore the skin right off my hand." She looked at her palm, studying it. "You never know what a wild animal will do." Her voice sounded more like the old Aunt Corinne. This was the most she'd said to me since I arrived.

The sound of another knock jarred me. "Now who is it?" she snapped. The witch was back.

My aunt yanked open the wooden door. On the other side of the screen was a mailman. He was tall and thin and had a nice, friendly face.

"Hello, Corinne," he said with a smile. "I heard ya been feelin' a little under the weather, so I thought I'd drop yer mail by for ya. Cards ain't nearly as much fun after Christmas."

He was right about that. Sometimes I get a birthday card after my birthday and it's just not the same. Aunt Corinne finally opened the screen door and took the cards. "Thank you," she said, then closed the door and went through the kitchen into the living room. I followed her. She walked slowly to the rocking chair, sat down and rocked a bit. She looked at the stack of cards in her hands for a long time before she gently opened the first one and read it. She blinked away tears, tucked the card back into the envelope and stood up. She went over to the fireplace, dropped the cards into the flames and headed back to her room.

I watched as the crackling flames turned the envelopes brown. Then they curled up and disappeared into ash. I wondered who had sent them.

I don't know how long I stood there but it must have been quite a while. It was like the flames were hypnotizing me. I shook my head to clear it and looked around the empty room. What was I going to do?

From out of nowhere, a bright beam of sunlight streamed through the window. It made the room look beautiful. I felt a sudden urge to go for a walk. And since I don't get that urge very often, I decided to go with it.

I grabbed a bag of chips, pulled on my gloves and plunked my stupid-looking hat on my head. Then I started walking. No place in particular, just walking. After about five minutes, I saw a hill and went to check out what was on the other side. As I climbed, I was surprised to see another white plastic bag float by. What were the chances of two plastic bags floating around like that? It had to be the one from yesterday.

I watched as it danced along the ground, then filled with air and twirled a few times. At one point it hovered right in front of my face. I could actually see inside. I tried to grab it but it jerked away. I grabbed again. Still no luck. The bag stayed just out of reach. All of a sudden a strong gust of wind blew it up the side of the hill. As it rose, I gave it a little good-bye wave. When it reached the top, a hand grabbed it!

A boy about my age stood right at the top of the hill. He looked pale, sort of washed out, like a really old T-shirt. He looked at me but didn't say anything, just waved and disappeared over the crest of the hill.

That was odd.

I was still staring at the hill when black clouds came over the top of it. The light around me grew darker as the clouds passed overhead. They were moving really fast. It looked creepy. When they completely covered the sun, the wind picked up and a flash of lightning streaked across the sky. The thunder that followed shook the ground. It really shook it!

I raced down the hill but there was no way I could outrun the storm. Within a couple of seconds, I was inside a whiteout. I couldn't see a thing.

# 7

If I kept running, I'd have probably tripped or crashed into something, so I stopped dead. It was weird standing there, not being able to see. All I could hear was the sound of the wind.

Then I thought I heard someone whisper, "Joey."

My head jerked to the right but all I saw was the wall of snow. "Hello?"

"Joey."

"Who's there?!" I took a few steps in the direction of the voice.

Suddenly, a car drove by me. I yelled and threw myself to the ground. The sound of the engine faded away. What idiot would be driving in this storm?!

As fast as it came, the storm passed. I quickly looked around to see who had called my name. No one was there. I got up feeling a little shaky and headed home. Near the house, it started to snow again but it was regular flakes this time. I could see just fine.

In the porch, I took off my hat and boots and went into the living room. I didn't turn on the light, just walked over to the couch in front of the window and watched snow swirl against the pane. A few minutes later it turned to ice, making loud, sharp tapping sounds. In two days it'd be Christmas. I'd never felt so lonely in my whole life.

Sliding down, I pulled the large pillows around me and listened to the ice hitting the window. As I fell asleep I thought about the boy I'd seen on the hill. Was he the one who had called my name?

When I woke up, the room was dark and cold. The fire must have gone out. Even though my face felt cold, my body was cozy and warm under the pillows. I felt really hungry and I knew I should get up but I was way too comfortable. As I tried to convince myself to move, I heard Aunt Corinne's bedroom door creak. I couldn't see anything but I heard my aunt slowly make her way down the hall. Once she got to the living room, she walked faster and pushed open the kitchen door.

Then I heard the back door close. She was gone again.

I sent the pillows flying, pushed through the kitchen door and grabbed my coat. I pulled on my boots, stuck on my hat and stepped outside, holding the screen door while it closed so that it wouldn't make any sound.

As I bolted down the steps, my feet slipped. I yelled and caught hold of the railing in time. The sound wasn't loud enough to be heard over the ice pellets hitting the ground.

Aunt Corinne was pretty far ahead of me, but I could see by the light from her lantern. The hill was covered in snow and I kept slipping on the icy patches. I started walking in shuffling steps and felt really dumb — lucky nobody could see me. As if anybody in their right mind would be out on a night like this. Aunt Corinne wasn't in her right mind, that's for sure. She was crazy, just like the people at the coffee shop said. Where would a crazy person go on such a horrible night?

The howling wind whipped the ice right into my face. I squinted so the pellets wouldn't poke me in the eyes and held my arm in front of my face for protection.

Aunt Corinne was heading for town. What could be open so late? Maybe she was going to somebody's house. But whose? And why? I really hate it when things don't make sense.

Where the road curved, I lost sight of her. I started running but when I got around the curve, Aunt Corinne was gone, disappeared into thin air. Then I saw the lantern. Aunt Corinne was heading toward the cliff. But why? I could only think of one answer — my aunt was going to jump. She was going to kill herself!

# 8

Aunt Corinne crossed a wooden bridge and turned left — definitely heading toward the ocean. A bright light swept across the sky. What was going on? Then I remembered — the lighthouse. Within a few minutes my aunt reached it. There it stood, at least three stories high, built into the side of the hill. It looked like it was growing out of the rocks. I stayed behind a bush and watched as my aunt knocked on the door. A couple of seconds later it opened and she went inside. I noticed a light coming from a window about a third of the way up. The rocks led right to it. Should I climb up? Would I be able to see inside? As I stood there deciding what to do, two beams of light appeared behind me, hovering in midair.

As they got closer, I realized they were headlights. I scrambled up the rocks at the side of the lighthouse, hid in the shadows and watched as a black van came to a stop. A guy with a long coat stepped out. Then I heard an electric machinery kind of sound and saw an old man in a wheelchair slowly coming out the side of the van. The man had white hair and a white beard. When the wheelchair reached the ground, the sound stopped. The younger guy put up the old man's hood to protect him from the ice and pushed the wheelchair off the ramp. The ramp folded itself back into the van and the side panel shut. The two men moved out of sight toward the lighthouse door. I heard voices and the door closing. The headlights shut off and everything went dark again.

A dull light came from the window above me. I peeked in but couldn't see anything. When I stretched a little higher, I leaned against the window and the frame moved — the window wasn't locked.

As the lighthouse beam swept across the ocean, I pried open the window. It didn't make a sound.

I poked my head inside and saw a winding staircase that went all the way from the bottom of the lighthouse to the top. Below, I could see some people standing around talking, but the wind was too loud to hear what they were saying. I knew if I kept the window open much longer they'd feel the cold air, so I took a deep breath, climbed inside and pulled the window shut.

A sturdy wooden platform led from the window to the staircase. I inched my way along but suddenly the platform creaked. My heart stopped. Just then there was a knock at the door.

"That must be Jana," a woman's voice said. "She called last night and said she was coming."

Someone must have opened the door because the wind howled loudly enough for me to move over to the stairs and sit down without being heard. I could see perfectly.

The woman who opened the door was tall with long gray hair and she was wearing a green shawl. My aunt sat in a chair against the wall, staring down at her hands, and the young guy was tucking a plaid blanket around the knees of the old man in the wheelchair. A third man, with a dark mustache, leaned against a panel of red and green blinking lights.

I heard the lady named Jana say, "Wretched weather. I almost didn't come. Thought maybe you'd cancel."

"Wouldn't dream of it." The lady with the long hair helped Jana off with her coat. "This is Corinne Simmonds." I heard Jana say hello but I didn't hear my aunt respond. "You know Mr. Halley and David." Both men said hello. "And this is my cousin Eli. He'll be joining us tonight."

"It's almost midnight, Elizabeth." My aunt stood up and walked over to a round table in the middle of the room. The floor had a black circle painted on it and the table sat inside the circle. Aunt Corinne pulled out a chair.

"Let's get started then, shall we?" Elizabeth slipped off her shawl and placed it over the panel of blinking lights. David pushed the old man's wheelchair in beside Aunt Corinne, pulled out a chair for Jana and then sat down beside her.

Elizabeth's cousin, Eli, limped slowly across the room and sat on the other side of Aunt Corinne. That left one seat empty. Elizabeth took out what looked like a thin black stick from a purple bowl on a small shelf. She lit the end of the stick with a match and circled the room, waving the stick and mumbling something. A thin stream of smoke hung in the air behind her, and a strong smell drifted up to me. I didn't like it.

When Elizabeth had completely circled the table, she put the stick back in the bowl and flicked out the lights. The lighthouse was plunged into total darkness. My stomach lurched. What was going on? I heard a scratching sound and a flame appeared. Elizabeth lit a candle on a tall iron stand, then lit two more. The flickering lights cast an eerie glow around the room, like something out of a horror movie.

She sat down in the empty chair. "Please join hands," she said. "Left palm up, right palm down." Everyone clasped hands with the person on either side. Elizabeth took a breath and slowly said, "Relax ... close your eyes ... still your mind."

She looked at each face and then closed her eyes, too. Everything stayed quiet until I heard her say, "I welcome my spirit guides as we gather here on holy ground and ask them to call forth the spirits of our loved ones. Our hearts are open. We wish to connect."

Elizabeth was breathing in and out pretty loud but nothing happened for a really long time. "Are there any spirits here wishing to communicate?"

Spirits? *Here?*

More silence. Even longer this time. My legs were getting cramped and the smell from the burning stick was making me really sick when, all of a sudden, the smell changed. It turned sweet. Like a room full of flowers.

"Lilacs," said Mr. Halley, and he smiled. "Evelyn's favorite."

Elizabeth smiled, too. "Evelyn says that through her eyes flowers are more beautiful than you can imagine."

Who was Evelyn?

"She's laughing," Elizabeth said. "Says you are the sweetest husband a woman could ask for."

Who said he was the sweetest husband?

"She's laughing because you're still leaving the porch light on for her."

"I know she's coming home, that's why!" chuckled Mr. Halley. "Tell her ... tell her."

"She hears you, Mr. Halley. And she says maybe someday, but not just yet."

Mr. Halley's smile faded. He nodded his head sadly.

An even longer silence followed. I thought Elizabeth had fallen asleep. But then she faced Jana and, with her eyes still closed, said, "Robert's here."

Jana's face lit up.

"He says to stop worrying about him. He feels *wonderful*. The sun is always shining. And the light — oh, the light is so incredible! So brilliant!"

I glanced around. Robert? There was no Robert in the room. Something strange was going on.

Jana smiled. Then she started crying softly.

"He wants to know if Sarah's sleeping through the night."

Jana gave a little laugh. "Yes. And in her own bed, too."

"He told you she would," said Elizabeth.

"Yes, yes he did." Jana smiled.

"He wants you to tell her that, if she gets scared, all she has to do is —" Elizabeth stopped talking. Her head began to turn from side to side as if she was scanning some scene.

"Robert! Please bring him back!" Jana pleaded.

"Someone's coming," said Elizabeth.

She breathed even more deeply. Then her head tilted back. It's a good thing her eyes were shut or she would have spotted me for sure.

Suddenly, her head snapped forward. I saw her arms stiffen and her whole body started jerking. Was she sick? Was she having a heart attack? Nobody moved. I was about to shout "Do something!" when Elizabeth's eyes popped open and the most evil-sounding voice came out of her mouth. "Beware the shadow of death! The shadow of death comes!"

I screamed. Losing my balance, I went crashing down the stairs. Everyone jumped up and looked at me. I scrambled to my feet and flew out the door. I had to get away from the lighthouse, away from the devil!

# 9

The ground was uneven and seemed icier than before. I fell a couple of times in the dark but nothing was going to stop me from getting away. Nothing. Suddenly my feet got caught in some wire and I stumbled forward — right into a fence. A nail scratched my hand and I felt blood trickle down my wrist. Where had that fence come from? That's when I realized I'd veered off the road — the only way I knew to get home.

I followed the wire and posts and finally spotted the road up ahead. I glanced back and saw light pouring out the open door of the lighthouse. The van engine revved. The headlights snapped on. They were coming after me.

The lights danced as the van drove over the rough road. I dropped to the ground and watched it pass. A couple of seconds later, I heard its tires on the wooden bridge and headed toward the sound, running and running until I finally got to the main road.

I made my way back to the house and rushed inside. No use taking off my boots — I wasn't planning on staying. I ran straight to my bedroom, yanked my suitcase out of the closet and jammed some sweaters and jeans inside. Then, like a bolt of lightning, it hit me. Why had I come back *here?* It's the *first* place they'd look! Get out! my brain screamed. Get out, fast!

Headlights shone through the window. Too late! The van pulled up beside the house. If I didn't make a sound, they might think I wasn't here. No. I couldn't take the chance. I pushed the heavy dresser in front of the door.

There were sounds of muffled voices, then the lights swept across the wall again. The van was pulling away. Good. Good.

"Joey!"

Aunt Corinne's footsteps neared my door. What was I going to do?

"Joey!"

A knock and then the door opened. It banged up against the dresser. "I know you're there," said my aunt. "Please let me come in?" Her voice was soft and kind, but she was a witch and no witch was getting in my room. "Please, Joey? I want to explain."

"Stay away from me!"

"I know you're scared and upset. What you saw at the lighthouse must have frightened you but I can explain. *Really* I can."

"No!" I screamed. "Get away from me!"

She tried the door again. This time the dresser moved a little. I had to get out of there. *Fast*. I tried to open the window but it wouldn't go. Aunt Corinne pushed the door again, harder. The dresser moved even more. I tried the window again. It still wouldn't budge. *Why?* Then I remembered the catch that swung around to unlock it. I slid the catch in a half circle and up went the window. Swinging my legs over the ledge, I jumped to the ground. It was all ice and I fell hard, hitting my elbow. Scrambling to my feet, I headed down the hill.

I don't know how I got to town, but suddenly I was walking along the deserted street. A quick movement caught my eye. I turned my head and saw a man standing in a doorway. My stomach tightened. It was too dark to make out his face but his eyes were bright — and they were staring right at me.

I felt scared but I tried to act casual, as if walking through town in the middle of the night was a normal thing to do. I even started whistling.

Don't ask me why, but I did. Then I glanced over my shoulder. The man was following me!

I moved faster. So did he. As his footsteps got closer, I panicked and started to run flat out. I passed a lot of stores and turned down a side street. Only it wasn't a street, it was an alley. With a sickening feeling I realized there was no way out.

As the dark figure came around the corner, I shouted, "Who are you? What do you want?!"

It moved toward me. I backed up.

"You tell on me and I'll bite your eye," the man shouted in a high-pitched voice, waving a bottle around. "You heard me. I'll bite your eye. So just keep your mouth shut!" With that, he ran off.

My body relaxed a little. It was just some drunk, acting crazy.

I moved farther into the shadows where nobody could see me. What was I going to do? What *could* I do?

Cry. That's what I did. Cried like a baby.

When the crying stopped, I looked around. The alley was sheltered from the wind but I knew it was too cold to stay there all night. My hands were stinging like crazy, so I jammed them into my pockets and that's when

I felt it — Harry's card! My mind started racing. I had to find a phone. Think. Think. Coffee shops! There's always a phone near a coffee shop!

I jumped up, made my way to the end of the alley and peered out. The street was empty. I headed out. The coffee shop that Harry had taken me to wasn't far — and I was right. Just around the corner from it stood an old-fashioned wooden phone booth. Slipping a quarter into the slot, I listened for the tone and then dialled. "Please answer," I begged. "Please answer."

"Hello?" Harry sounded sleepy.

"Harry! Something bad's happened and I don't know what to do!"

"Joey? Is that you?"

"Yes!"

"What's happened?"

"Please come and get me."

"Just hold on tight. I won't be but a minute."

"Harry, I'm not at Aunt Corinne's!"

"Where are you?"

"In town. Beside the coffee shop. At the phone booth."

"What on earth? Never mind. Stay right there. I'm on my way."

I stayed and waited. Harry was taking forever and I was frozen solid. Finally I saw headlights. My heart almost burst with joy. I tore out of the phone booth waving both arms so Harry could see me. But as the van stopped, I realized it wasn't Harry. It was the black van from the lighthouse!

# 10

I took off screaming. Looking back, I saw the van turning around — it was coming after me! I ducked into the dark doorway of the hardware store, where there was a little alcove, and crouched down low. The headlights slowly approached. I hid my face in my arms so I'd blend into the darkness. The van drove right past me. I didn't look up until I couldn't hear the engine anymore.

Too afraid to move, I stayed crouched against the door until a horn honked. Had the van come back?

Then I heard Harry's voice. "Joey! Joey!"

I jumped up and raced down the street. There was Harry standing by the phone booth. I was never so happy to see anyone in my whole life. I threw my arms around him.

"Sorry I took so long, Joey. I couldn't find the darn keys." Harry patted my back. "What's happened? What are you doin' here?"

"Could we go home?" My voice was barely a whisper.

"Of course."

When we got in the van, I pounded down the lock. Harry drove down the street and then headed the van toward Aunt Corinne's house.

"Nooo!"

Harry slammed on the brakes. "What's *wrong?*"

"Not Aunt Corinne's! Please, Harry!"

"Joey, what's —"

"Not *there!*"

"All right. All right." Harry tried to keep his voice calm. "We'll go to *my* house. Is that okay?"

I nodded. "Yes. Thank you."

Harry turned the van around. About five minutes later, we pulled into a driveway next to a green two-story wooden house with a white picket fence. As we walked up the steps, I noticed a nativity scene in the front yard. Baby Jesus didn't have it so easy either.

The door swung open. A short, chubby woman stood there in her bathrobe. As soon as I saw her, I wanted her to wrap her arms around me.

"You must be Joey." She smiled. "I'm Maxine, Harry's wife. Come in," she said, just like she was expecting me. Adults usually give each other those looks that they think kids don't catch, but she didn't.

Maxine helped me off with my coat, just like my mom used to when I was a little kid. Then she put her arm around my shoulder and led me into the living room. "Come on, sweetheart." She must have felt me shivering because she pulled a blanket off a rocking chair and wrapped it around me. "There, that should warm you up a bit." She sat me in an armchair. "I'll go make us somethin' hot to drink. Would you like that?"

I nodded.

Harry came over and sat on the edge of the coffee table. "Do you want to tell me what happened tonight, Joey?"

Of course I wanted to tell him. I wanted to scream it out, but the words wouldn't come.

"If you have somethin' to say, speak up. A closed mouth doesn't get fed."

Okay. I stared Harry right in the eyes. "My aunt's a witch."

Harry started to laugh. Then he saw the look on my face and stopped.

"Not the kind with a pointy hat and a broomstick," I said, my voice sounding hard. "The kind that acts mean and yells and goes to lighthouses in the middle of the night and sits in the dark with other witches."

Harry's brow creased. "Corinne took you to the lighthouse?" He sounded angry. "What was she thinking?"

"She didn't take me. I followed her."

"How on earth did you get inside?"

"I crawled through a window. Then I listened from the stairs. She's a witch. They're all witches."

"Your aunt's not a witch," said Harry firmly. "Let's get that straight right off the bat."

"Well, one of the ladies was. She closed her eyes and talked like she was on the phone. Like she could hear somebody but nobody else could. Then she'd say what the person said, only that person wasn't there!"

"This lady? Tall with long gray hair, was she?"

"Yes!"

Harry nodded. "Elizabeth Duff. I swear to you, Joey, she's not a witch. She's a psychic and a channeler."

"What's that?"

Harry thought for a minute before he answered. "A psychic communicates with spirits of people who have passed on. And a channeler is a person who allows the spirit of someone who's died to enter them and speak through them."

I couldn't believe what I was hearing. Was Harry kidding?

"Both are ways of communicatin' directly with a loved one who's ... died. Elizabeth has a gift."

"Having someone *dead* inside you is a *gift?*"

"I know it sounds —"

"Dead people don't talk!" I shouted.

"You're right. You're right. But some people believe that their ... spirits live on and ... sometimes those spirits can communicate if they have someone to communicate *through*. That's where Elizabeth comes in. She's been holdin' séances at the lighthouse for years. Her grandparents were the lighthouse keepers. And her great-grandmother —" Harry suddenly stopped.

"What, Harry?"

He shook his head. "Nothin' ... nothin'."

"Her great-grandmother *what?* Tell me." I was half pleading, half demanding.

"It'll just upset you."

"Say it, Harry."

Harry took a breath. "She was a sea witch."

"I told you!" I shouted. "They're all witches!"

"It's just an expression, son. It doesn't mean the kind of witch you're thinkin'. In the old days, when a sailor died at sea, his wife would call on a sea witch to come to her home and try to contact the spirit of her dead husband."

"One in a million has the gift," said Maxine, carrying in a wooden tray.

There was that word again. If I had that gift, I'd give it back.

The tray had three mugs of steaming hot chocolate on it. Harry handed me one and took one for himself. I guess Harry's help always came with hot chocolate.

"Elizabeth's had the gift since she was a child." Maxine sat on the couch beside my chair. "It seems to be strongest when she's at the lighthouse. Some energy around it or in it makes contact easier."

This was starting to sound like *The X-Files*.

"Did your uncle come through?" asked Harry.

"Through what?"

"Sorry. Did your uncle speak to your aunt through Elizabeth?"

"No." I swallowed hard. "But the devil did."

The crease between Harry's eyes deepened. "What do you mean, Joey?"

"It was the most evil voice I've ever heard, Harry."

"And the voice came through Elizabeth?" Maxine sounded worried and surprised.

I nodded.

Harry leaned in. "What did it say? Tell me the exact words."

"It said, 'Beware the shadow of death! The shadow of death comes!'" I said it the way it sounded in that deep, gravelly voice.

Harry looked shaken. "Something must have gone wrong."

"What do you mean *wrong?*"

I suddenly had a really bad feeling that Harry and Maxine were witches. They knew way too much about all this creepy stuff.

"Once in a while," Harry said quietly, "*very* rarely, a spirit will come through that's not been invited."

"You open yourself up when you're channeling," said Maxine. "Evil spirits hover around sometimes just waitin' for an opening."

How would she know? Was she one?

"Usually a prayer of protection keeps them away," she added.

Prayer had to be good. Evil spirits wouldn't pray.

"Did Elizabeth say a prayer before she started?" Harry asked.

"I ... I don't remember anything that sounded like a prayer. She said some words when she was walking around the table, but I didn't hear anything about God or anything."

"It surprises me that something negative like that would slip through." Harry shook his head. "The lighthouse is a holy place."

"Have you been there?"

A shadow fell over Harry's face. Maxine's too. "Our son died. Remember, Joey — I told you about him at the coffee shop."

I nodded.

"He was twelve," Maxine said. "When someone you love is taken away suddenly, you become desperate — you have to know that they're okay, that they're safe and happy. I can't explain, but ..."

"I think I understand."

Maxine's eyes held mine for a long moment. "Some people thought I was crazy, and I *was*. Crazy with pain. Elizabeth was a great help to me, a real comfort. Harry didn't believe at first, but he was willin' to give it a try." She smiled at him. "So one night we met Elizabeth at the lighthouse."

"Elizabeth channeled our son," said Harry. "I'd know Samuel's sweet voice anywhere. It came through clear as a bell, like he was right here in the room. He said he was doin' fine. All the pain was gone. He told us not to be sad ... to go on with our lives." Harry's eyes shone like he was somewhere else. A good place. "He told us we didn't need to keep going to the graveyard because he wasn't there."

Maxine had the same look in her eyes. "He'd become the morning sun and the evening breeze ... the river ... the woods. He was part of all living things."

A peace settled over me like a warm blanket.

"Communicatin' with Samuel made our lives livable again," said Harry softly. "Your aunt's heart is still filled with pain over losin' your Uncle Stephen. That's why she went to the lighthouse. I don't know what voice came through, but I don't think it was Stephen. He was a kind and gentle man."

Maxine rubbed my arm. "I'm sorry, Joey. It must'a been real frightenin'."

"I don't want to go back to Aunt Corinne's," I whispered. "Please don't make me go back."

Maxine looked at Harry, then at me. "You can stay here with us till we sort this out."

"Of course," said Harry. "I'll call Corinne and tell her —"

"No! Don't tell her where I am!"

Harry looked startled. "I have to let her know you're okay, Joey. She'll be worried sick."

"Just don't let her take me away. Please, Harry? Promise me."

"I promise. I won't let that happen."

"Come on darlin'," Maxine said, taking my hand. "Let's get you to bed."

I followed her up the stairs to a small bedroom full of boys' stuff. Had to be Samuel's.

"The first door on your right's the bathroom," said Maxine. "I'll leave the light on so you can find it." She pulled open a drawer and lifted out a pair of blue striped pajamas. "I never could bring myself to give away Samuel's things. I know it's silly, but I take comfort in keepin' things the way they were."

Sizzle! Pop! Out went the light!

I gasped.

"Shoot," said Maxine. "I told Harry to get bulbs when he was in town. That man would forget 'is head if it weren't attached." She laughed and flicked on a lamp. The shade was stained glass and the light made the colors glow.

"That's really pretty."

"Samuel made it. He had a real creative streak, he did. Loved doin' artistic things." She smiled. "Your Aunt Corinne's light has gone out. Just like that darn bulb. But it'll come back. I promise. Good night, Joey."

After Maxine left, I put on Samuel's pajamas, turned out his lamp and crawled into his bed. I stared into the darkness, thinking. It all seemed like a dream, not real life. I tossed and turned and listened to the clock tick away ... doing its job ... not worrying about anything ... not afraid. The wind rattled the window.

# 11

A slice of morning sun hit me right in the face.
I got up, pulled back the curtains and stared at
the beautiful sunrise. Hello, Samuel.

A delicious baking smell drifted into the room.
It made me smile. I was in a safe place with kind
people who cared about me — and I was going to
get to eat. For the first time in days, I wasn't afraid.

I threw on my clothes and did a little hop
along the hall. Skipping down the stairs, I swung
around the doorframe into the living room.

Aunt Corinne was sitting there looking at me.

"What're you doing here?" I glared at her.
"Harry!" I ran into the kitchen. "Maxine! Harry!"

The back door opened and Harry stepped in,
his face red from the cold.

"Where were you?" I said, sounding angrier
than I'd meant to.

"Just saltin' the driveway. I don't want anyone
to fall on that ice, especially me."

"I thought you were gone."

"I wouldn't go without tellin' you first."

"She's here, Harry. In the living room."

"I know, son. She came first thing this mornin'. Said she felt real bad about last night and wanted to talk to you."

"I don't want to go back with her. *Please,* Harry. Don't make me." I was whining but I couldn't help it.

"You don't have to do anything you don't want to do. Just let your aunt explain. That's all I ask."

I didn't want to hear anything Aunt Corinne had to say. "Come with me?"

"I'll be right here, Joey. Maxine's gone to visit her sister in the hospital, but she gave me detailed instructions on how to put the icin' on these here Christmas cookies. I'll get down to it while you listen to your aunt. Okay?"

I thought it over. "Okay ... But I'm *not* going home with her."

"Understood."

I headed back to the living room.

Aunt Corinne's eyes were red and swollen. She'd been crying, but I didn't feel sorry for her.

"I'm not going home with you. And you can't make me."

My aunt nodded. "Being with me is probably the last thing you want. I understand ... and I would never force you."

"Then what are you doing here?"

She looked down at her hands. "After you left last night, I had a lot of time to think. It was the first time in months I thought about somebody besides myself." Her voice trembled. So did her hands. "I'm so ashamed. I've been selfish and cruel. I don't blame you for hating me."

"I don't hate you, Aunt Corinne ... But I don't like you anymore."

She nodded again and dabbed a tissue on her swollen eyes. "I've been up all night thinking about you — how angry you must feel. How scared you must be. And it's all my fault." Her voice caught. "I've been so awful to you. How could I have treated you so badly? What was I thinking? What kind of person have I become?" She shook her head. "I'm sorry, Joey. So *very* sorry."

Her body began to shake, then tears poured out. I didn't know what to do, so I just listened to her cry.

"I miss your Uncle Stephen *so* much." She leaned forward holding her stomach. "I had to talk to him one last time."

"He's *dead*. You can't talk to somebody who's dead!"

"But sometimes, if you —"

"Uncle Stephen is *dead!*"

"I know he is, but I needed to try. Just one word ... that's all I wanted." Tears kept rolling down her face. "It hurts so much. Sometimes I don't think I can go on. I don't *want* to go on." She started to rock back and forth.

My aunt didn't seem like a witch anymore, just a person who had lost somebody she loved, and there wasn't anything she could do about it. I remembered how bad it felt when my dad left my mom and me.

"I miss my dad." My words came out in a whisper. "I want to talk to him all the time, but he never calls." My throat suddenly felt tight. I could barely breathe. My aunt's eyes looked even sadder. But this time they were sad for me. I slowly walked over and sat down beside her. She wrapped her arms around me and pulled me close. I heard her whisper, "I'm sorry, Joey. Please forgive me."

Her pain seemed to mix with mine. "I forgive you."

Harry drove us home. We didn't talk very much. I sat in the back with my head leaning against the window, looking out at the passing houses. Every tree, every bush was covered with shimmering ice. It didn't seem real and for a second I thought maybe I was dreaming. It was that beautiful.

As we turned out of town, we saw flashing red lights. An ambulance was heading our way. No siren, just red lights turning. Right behind it was the black van from last night.

"David's van," Harry said. "Something must have happened to John."

"He was there last night, Harry. He was at the *lighthouse!*"

"The man driving the van is David Halley," Aunt Corinne said. "He takes his grandfather to visit Elizabeth once in a while. They're good people, honey."

"They are, Joey. I've known old John for over forty years," said Harry as he turned onto the road leading up to the house. "Wonderful man." Then he sighed. "Last year he and the missus were drivin' home late when their car skidded on some black ice and crashed. John broke his back. He's been in a wheelchair ever since."

"Did Mrs. Halley die?" I asked.

Harry shook his head. "No. But good as dead, if ya ask me."

"She's in a coma," said Aunt Corinne.

"So if she's not dead, why does he go see Elizabeth?"

Harry changed gears to get up the hill. "John believes that his wife's spirit has left her body and is hoverin' around in some form."

"I don't want to scare you," said my aunt. "But I believe she communicates with him ... through Elizabeth. I've heard her, several times. Elizabeth tells Mr. Halley things that only he and his wife could possibly know about — private things."

"It's probably a trick." I didn't want to believe spirits could wander around outside their bodies.

Aunt Corinne smiled. "A lot of people would agree with you." She patted my arm.

As Aunt Corinne and I walked up the porch steps, she asked, "Are you hungry?"

"Starving."

Inside the kitchen she stopped and crinkled her nose. "It smells funny in here."

"It smells bad, Aunt Corinne."

"You're right." She picked up the garbage, dumped it in a bag and flung it into a metal can outside. Then she did the same with the garbage under the sink. "Now, let's see. What can we scrounge up to eat around here?"

"Nothing. I've looked." I didn't want her to feel bad but it was the truth.

Aunt Corinne nodded her head. "I'm sorry, Joey."

"It's okay. I bought some Cheez Whiz and bread and peanut butter the other day. We can eat that."

Aunt Corinne managed a little smile, then brushed the hair off my face and tilted my chin up with her hand. "You're a terrific kid, you know that?"

"They don't come any better than me."

She laughed out loud.

After the bread and Cheez Whiz — and a can of baked beans we found at the back of a cupboard — we were both still hungry.

"We need to get some real food." It was as though Aunt Corinne had read my mind. "And a turkey, if they haven't sold out."

The temperature had continued to drop. As we listened to the radio we heard the announcer say that this was the coldest winter in years.

Aunt Corinne looked out the kitchen window. "It's never been this cold. *Never.*"

She reached for the phone. "I hate to bother Harry again but we'll be frozen stiff if we walk."

Harry was at our door in twenty minutes.

In town, Aunt Corinne went for groceries, Harry headed to the coffee shop, and I set off looking for something nice to buy my aunt for Christmas. I still had twenty dollars left. We agreed to meet Harry in half an hour.

There weren't many places to buy presents, so I walked over to the antique shop. Fake snow had been sprayed on one corner of each window pane. I put my face close to the glass and looked inside. There were old-fashioned sleighs and angels and some wooden toys. Then I saw a reflection in the window. It was a boy playing with a yo-yo. When he saw me looking at him, he waved. I realized it was the same boy who'd been on the hill yesterday and turned around to talk to him. An old man walked by, but the boy wasn't there. Where did he go? I looked up and down the street. He wasn't anywhere.

I shrugged and turned back to the antique shop. Maybe there was something inside that Aunt Corinne would like. As I stepped into the store, a bell tinkled. I held the door for an old lady on her way out and the bell tinkled again as the door closed.

"Finally! She's gone," I heard someone say and then a curtain slid open. Out stepped a tall man with curly brown hair. He was wearing blue baggy pants and a large red work shirt with a huge lady's brassiere over it. "What'd ya think, Patrick?" he asked the man behind the counter.

That's when he spotted me, let out a yell and jumped back behind the curtain.

"You never saw nothin', right?" said Patrick with a smile.

"Right," I answered. He nodded and laughed.

I went down some aisles checking out the old dishes and vases. Along the far wall, I saw a painting. It was of an angel looking really angry. On the gold-colored frame was the title, "Fall from Grace."

"This here's the archangel who turned against God."

I spun around. It was the man who was dressed funny — only now he had on jeans and a sweater. "We know him as ..." He leaned in and whispered, "*The devil.*"

"Don't scare the boy, Jack," said Patrick.

"It takes more than that to scare me," I said. After hearing the devil with my own ears, a painting was nothing.

"Then allow me to show you somethin' that gave me a few nightmares," Jack said. We went down an aisle and over to a dark cabinet. "This here armoire belonged to my granny," he said, indicating the cabinet. "She had five children but three of 'em died before they were ten years old. Caused her to go nutty, it did. The two kids still alive, my dad and his brother, were shipped off to an aunt's. Are you followin'?"

"Yup."

"Good. So, the aunt raised the two kids while Nan withered away in the nuthouse. They let her bring this armoire — it was the one thing she asked for." He ran his hand along the polished wood. "Kept it locked the whole time she was in the loony bin. When she died, it got passed on to me." He stared at the cabinet for a bit, then said, "Want to see what she kept inside?"

"Sure." I wasn't sure at all.

Jack grinned and slowly reached for the wooden knobs. In one quick motion, he swung open the doors and let out a loud scream. I froze at the sound and then let out my own scream. Five children sat on the shelf. It took me a couple of seconds to realize they weren't real, just dolls dressed in children's clothes. Their heads were all shrunken, with ugly wrinkled faces and beady, unblinking eyes.

"Guess she got her five kids back, eh?"

I was mad at Jack — that was a lousy trick and I wanted to pay him back. "The one on the left looks a bit like you."

"Smart ass," said Jack, with a grin.

As he started to close the doors, I noticed some letters scratched into the wood just below the lock ... UMBRA RISUS

"It means 'Get me the heck out of here!'" Jack laughed. "Actually, if my days in Father Bragg's Latin class serve me, it means 'shadow of a smile.'"

"That's nice. Why'd she write it on the door?"

"Beats me how it got there, but Nan didn't write it. She couldn't write in English let alone Latin."

Jack closed the doors, patted my shoulder and walked off. Weird guy. I went back to looking around for something to buy Aunt Corinne.

In a small room off to the side, I found a stack of really nice books. One had a leather cover and the pages had gold along the edges. It came in its own box. *The Poems of Elizabeth Barrett Browning*. There wasn't any price on it, so I took it to the front counter to ask Patrick how much it cost.

"Elizabeth Barrett Browning — good choice."

He flipped through some pages. "She was once considered the female Shakespeare, you know." I guess that meant she was really talented. "I hate to part with it but ... I'll give it to you for, let's say, forty dollars."

My eyebrows shot up.

"I know that look," he said. "A little too rich for your blood?"

"A little too rich for my wallet," I replied. "Thanks anyway."

I searched a bit more but didn't find anything interesting that I could afford, so I headed for the door. As I went down a narrow aisle, my hip bumped a table and something fell on the floor. I almost tripped trying not to step on it. It was a flat wooden triangle with little feet on the bottom, and in the center was a small hole with an old-fashioned pen sticking out. I bent to pick it up and was surprised to see Patrick suddenly standing over me.

"That's a planchette," he said.

"How do you write with it?"

He gave a little laugh. "*You* don't do the writing. *It does*."

"It writes by itself?"

"It's, well, how can I put this? It's used by spirits to send messages from the afterlife ..."

My eyebrows shot up again.

"Or at least that's what it says on the box."

"Patrick is a skeptic." Where'd Jack come from? I didn't hear any footsteps. "If he can't see it with his own four eyes, he doesn't believe it. I, on the other hand, am a believer — tarot cards, psychic readings, automatic writing, tea leaves *and* this planchette."

He took the planchette from me and tightened one of the little feet. When he went to replace it on the table, he noticed that the paper it had been resting on had squiggly lines all over it. "Ah, the spirits have been around," he said, smiling.

Patrick shook his head. "If you can read what it says, I'll eat my hat."

"Let's see." Jack studied the lines. "Today's special ... two-for-one chicken lips." We all laughed.

"I believe," Jack went on, placing the planchette carefully on the paper, "that under the right circumstances, this thing's got powers we lowly humans can't begin to understand."

"How does it work?" I was actually curious about this thing.

"Sort of like a Ouija board, only instead of spellin' out words, it writes 'em." Jack placed his fingertips on top of the wood. "You gently rest your fingers on it and ask a question. Then you wait. If a spirit's in the neighborhood and in the mood, it'll write out an answer."

"How much does it cost?" I thought I'd never want to get near anything like this, but for some strange reason, I had to get it for Aunt Corinne.

"Today's your lucky day." Jack smiled. "It's on sale for the low, low price of twenty-five ninety-nine."

"Plus tax," piped in Patrick.

My heart sank. "I only have twenty dollars."

Jack rubbed his chin thoughtfully. "Do you have a cheque?"

"No."

"Credit card?"

"No."

"Then you're out of luck."

I thought Jack was kidding about that credit card stuff. I figured he'd give me a break. He didn't.

"We have a nice teapot in your price range," he said. "It once belonged to King Edward's second cousin, Louise, on his mother's side."

"I don't want a teapot. I want the planchette."

"Then you need to pony up another ten bucks. Right, Patrick?"

"Right."

There had to be a way around this. I thought really hard and then remembered something my friend Paul had shown me one night after seeing it in a movie. "How about a bet?"

Jack's right eyebrow went up. "Hmmm, what kind of bet?"

I made a circle by joining the tip of my thumb and the tip of my index finger. "I'll bet you ten dollars that I can poke my head through this hole."

Patrick rolled his eyes. "The boy's deluded."

"No, I'm not," I said. Whatever "deluded" meant.

"Okay," said Jack. "Let me get this straight. You're gonna poke your fat head through that iddy-biddy hole?"

I ignored the insult. "Yes."

"Okey dokey. You hand over ten bucks if you can't poke your head through the hole. We'll give you ten bucks off the price of the planchette if you can. Deal?"

"Deal."

Patrick crossed his arms. Jack squinted.

I took a deep breath, slowly lifted my hand and placed the finger circle against my forehead. Then, with my other hand, I tapped my forehead through the hole. Patrick looked surprised. Jack burst out laughing. "Ah, *that* kind of poke!"

Patrick shook his head. "Give 'im 'is planchette, Jack. It was worth it just to see how he'd do it."

# 12

Carrying the antique-store bag under my arm, I headed over to the coffee shop. When I opened the door, a terrific smell hit me in the face — sizzling bacon. Real food. I could practically taste it. I spotted Harry sitting at a table with Pete and his friends. As I neared them, a pretty waitress next to Harry stood up and said, "You must be Joey. Just sit yerself down. I was keepin' the seat warm for ya." She patted me on the shoulder. "Can I get you somethin' to eat?"

I was about to say "Bacon, eggs, toast, jam — everything" when I remembered I didn't have any money left. "No, thank you. I, um, already ate lunch."

Harry introduced me to everyone and then they went back to their conversation. "Has anybody heard if Mr. Halley's all right?" asked Pete.

"Must be," replied a lady. "They sent him home."

"So soon?"

She nodded. "My cousin Nora's daughter works at the hospital. She told Nora that the doctor thought Mr. Halley had a heart attack, but it was a false alarm."

"Wonder what brought it on?" asked Pete.

That evil voice, I thought. It practically gave *me* a heart attack. Harry spotted Aunt Corinne walking to the van. "There's Corinne. We'd better get goin'."

"Tell 'er to come in for a spell," said the waitress. "Haven't seen 'er in a dog's age."

"Maybe next time." Harry smiled. "It's her first day out and I think she's a wee bit tired."

Everyone wished us a Merry Christmas and out we went. Harry helped my aunt with her groceries and we climbed quickly into the van. As Harry started to back out, the black van appeared out of nowhere and Harry slammed on the brakes.

"There's David," said Aunt Corinne. "I wonder how his grandfather is."

"Back at home apparently," said Harry.

Aunt Corinne looked relieved. "Harry, you've been so generous with your time, and I really hate to ask, but would it be too much trouble to drop in on Mr. Halley? Just for a few minutes?"

"No trouble at all, Corinne."

My aunt turned around. "Is that okay with you, Joey?"

"With me? Sure." What choice did I have?

Five minutes later we arrived at Mr. Halley's red wooden house. Smoke curled out of the chimney. We walked slowly up the icy path and then Harry knocked on the door. A few seconds later, a woman with brown hair and a really long, sharp nose opened it.

"Hello, Mrs. Witter," said my aunt. "Is this a bad time to visit?"

"It's never a bad time when a friend comes to call." Smiling made her nose even longer.

We stepped inside, took off our boots and followed Mrs. Witter down a long hallway. As we got closer to a back room, we could hear a strange whirring sound.

Inside the room, the curtains were closed and it was pretty dark. Mr. Halley sat in his wheelchair staring at a large screen, and next to him was an old, noisy film projector. On the screen, a smiling lady with white curly hair was dancing with Mr. Halley. They both waved at the camera. Mrs. Witter gently tapped Mr. Halley's arm to get his attention. Then she said something to him and turned off the projector. The room went quiet. Aunt Corinne walked over to Mr. Halley and gently took one of his hands in hers.

"How are you feeling?"

Mr. Halley shook his head. "Not so good, Mrs. Simmonds. My heart is heavy." He began to cry. Quietly at first and then louder. Harry carried over a chair for my aunt. She sat down, never letting go of Mr. Halley's hand.

"Did that voice frighten you last night?" she asked softly.

"No ... no ..." he sobbed. "I know the voice. It was that terrible *message*. Evelyn's going to die."

Aunt Corinne looked surprised. That made two of us. "Mr. Halley," she said, "you recognized the voice?"

Mr. Halley nodded several times. "It was my brother, Harold. He died last year."

"That voice wasn't *human*, Mr. Halley." I couldn't stop myself. "How could it be your brother?"

Mr. Halley wiped his eyes and blew his nose on a white handkerchief. "I'll show you," he said. Then he reached up and turned the knob to reverse the film. We watched the screen as Mr. Halley and his wife quickly danced backward. Suddenly, a bunch of people were inside a restaurant. Mr. Halley stopped the film and turned the knob to "Play." The people were talking and wearing pointy hats, like kids do at birthday parties. Someone carried in a cake with lots of candles and everybody sang "Happy Birthday." The cake was placed in front of the man at the head of the table. "That's my brother. That's Harold," said Mr. Halley, pointing a gnarly finger at the screen. Then someone in the movie said, "Make a wish, Harold. And make it a good one." Everybody laughed.

Harold looked around the table. He smiled and said, "I have everything I need in life. Does anyone want my wish?" It was the voice we'd heard last night! The devil's voice!

Aunt Corinne looked really shaken and I had to sit down. Mr. Halley stopped the projector. "Harold smoked his whole life — ended up with throat cancer." He looked over at me. "The doctors had to remove his larynx. Where the vocal cords are." He pointed to his throat. "They replaced it with a voice box so he'd be able to speak. It sounds horrible, I know, but we got used to it."

Mr. Halley put his head down and stared at the floor. His eyes welled with tears. "Harold was

warning me, preparing me for Evelyn's death."
He leaned into Aunt Corinne. She tenderly put
her arm around him.

I felt really bad for Mr. Halley but relieved that
the voice wasn't Satan's. I didn't much like the
idea of Satan hanging around the neighborhood.

Back at home, Aunt Corinne and I walked up
the steps carrying the grocery bags. Suddenly, an
icicle from the edge of the roof crashed right at
our feet. Shards of ice flew in every direction.
We jumped back and our bags tumbled to the
ground.

"That was close," I said with a nervous laugh.

My aunt turned on me. "We could have
been killed!"

I instantly got a sick feeling in the pit of my
stomach. The witch was back again.

Aunt Corinne stared at the roof, where a long
row of icicles hung. Then, in a softer voice she
said, "I'll be glad to leave this godforsaken place."

She knelt down and started picking up the
groceries. She looked beaten again, like life was
just too hard.

As I helped her gather the food, she frowned.
"Something's missing." Then she spotted the

frozen turkey and gave a little laugh. "There it is." It had slid halfway across the yard.

After we carried everything inside, I went back out with a broom. As I swung at the icicles, I remembered seeing a movie once where an icicle fell straight on this guy's head. It was so sharp it went right through his skull. By the time they discovered his body, the icicle had melted and the police thought somebody had stabbed him in the head. Not too bright.

I gave the icicles a good whack. It felt great. Too bad I couldn't reach more of them.

When I went inside, Aunt Corinne seemed normal again. She had put the turkey in the sink to thaw and was making my favorite dinner — spaghetti with meat sauce and hot garlic bread.

After we ate, an amazing thing happened. My aunt watched TV with me — back-to-back episodes of *The Simpsons* — and she didn't say they were moronic, not even once. She even smiled a couple of times. Me, I practically peed myself laughing. For a dad, Homer's a bit of a goof. On the other hand, no matter what Bart does, Homer never walks out on him.

Back in the kitchen, my aunt and I had some apple pie. Then she asked if I wanted to play Snakes and Ladders.

"Sure. Why not?"

I got up and headed to the porch, where my aunt kept her board games. As I was pulling the Snakes and Ladders box from the top shelf, I heard a thump come from outside. I opened the door and looked through the screen. No one was there. A thick fog had set in. THUMP! The screen door shook. I jumped and saw the mangy cat that had been trying to get into the house earlier. I slammed the door. Why was that cat always trying to get into our house?

My aunt and I set up the board and played for a while, but I just couldn't concentrate. All I could think about was the planchette hidden under my bed.

"Aunt Corinne?"

"Yes?"

"Would you mind if I gave you your Christmas present tonight? Christmas Eve is *almost* Christmas."

"That'd be fine, honey," she said. "Lots of people open their gifts on Christmas Eve."

I ran to my bedroom and grabbed the bag. It was a nice one, so I didn't feel bad about not wrapping the present. Back in the kitchen, I handed it to my aunt like I was presenting her with a prize or something.

"Now, what could this be?" She took the bag and peeked inside, then pulled out the box and looked at the gold lettering. "A planchette!" She sounded surprised.

"Do you know what it is?"

"Haven't a clue." She grinned.

"Open it! I'll show you how it works."

Aunt Corinne lifted the lid and took out the triangle-shaped board.

"There's a pen in there, too ... and paper," I said.

I pushed the Snakes and Ladders out of the way while my aunt placed the planchette on the table. "It sits on top of the paper, Aunt Corinne." She lifted the planchette and slipped the paper under it. "And the pen fits in the hole."

My aunt slid the pen into the hole in the middle of the planchette. "Now what do you do?" she asked.

"Now you ask it questions. It *writes* out the answers. Maybe it can tell you if Uncle Stephen's ... okay."

My aunt looked up, surprised. "I — I thought you didn't believe in stuff like this."

I shrugged.

Aunt Corinne smiled and the lines around her eyes seemed to fade a little.

"Jack, the man at the antique shop, told me what to do. You rest your fingers gently on the board and ask a question."

"Sounds easy enough."

I sat down opposite my aunt. "Would you say a prayer of protection first?" I asked her. "I'd feel better." I didn't want any evil voices coming through again.

"Of course." She closed her eyes and took three long, deep breaths. Then she started her prayer. "May all present here be surrounded by iridescent light. We ask that only those that are of the light be allowed to enter this place." She slowly opened her eyes and smiled at me. "Ready, Joey?"

"Ready." I tried not to sound too nervous as I placed the fingers of both hands on my side of the planchette. Aunt Corinne did the same on hers. She breathed deeply again several times ... in and out, in and out. I found myself breathing in rhythm with her. Finally, she said, "Stephen, if you are anywhere near us, we welcome you."

She continued breathing deeply. "It would mean so much if you could just let me know that you're all right." More breathing and waiting ... waiting. Nothing happened. Aunt

Corinne cleared her throat. "If any entity of the light is here, please show us that you are present."

We waited some more. Still nothing happened. I kept my eyes focused on the pen, wishing with all my might that it would move. It didn't. I closed my eyes and concentrated on making that pen move. I heard Aunt Corinne say, "You are most welcome here. Please ... make yourself known."

An even longer silence followed. Finally I opened one eye and peeked at my aunt. Even though her eyes were closed, I saw a tear roll down her cheek.

I felt awful. I shouldn't have bought this stupid planchette. All it was doing was creating more pain, and Aunt Corinne already had more than her share. I started to pull my fingers away when I saw the pen move!

# 13

My gasp startled Aunt Corinne. Her eyes sprang open.

"It moved!" I said breathlessly. "I swear! I saw it move!"

Well, it wasn't moving now. Please ... move again ... move ... move. I concentrated so hard my head started hurting. And then the pen moved! It *really* did! And the board moved along with it, hovering over the paper.

My hands started shaking. Aunt Corinne looked at me pleadingly. I knew she didn't want my shaking to ruin what was happening. I tried to steady my hands and kept saying *Stay calm, stay calm* inside my head.

The planchette moved slowly and smoothly but the pen made little jerking motions. It was definitely writing something but we couldn't see anything. When the planchette reached the edge of the page it *flew* across the table, hit the counter and crashed to the floor. I yelled but Aunt Corinne stayed really calm. She stared at the paper and then slowly reached out and turned it around to face her. I jumped out of my chair. There was something written on it — sort of.

I looked at my aunt. "What the heck is that?"

"I don't know, Joey," she said. Then she sighed. "I hoped so hard that Stephen would say something to me."

"What a scam," I snapped. The lousy piece of wood wrote gibberish and it cost me twenty bucks. "It's just a piece of junk."

"No, Joey. Something *was* here. I could feel it. When the pen was writing, didn't you feel an energy flow through your fingers?"

I knew she wanted me to say yes. "Sorry. I didn't feel anything. Just scared."

"Something *was* here," she insisted. "The planchette moved on its own! How do you think it got on the floor?!"

I didn't like the edge in her voice.

A loud car horn honked. Then, I swear, it played "Yankee Doodle." Aunt Corinne's eyes widened. "Uh-oh."

"What's wrong?"

"She's here!"

"Who's here?"

"Stephen's *mother!* Hide it, Joey!" She pointed to the planchette. "Hide it!"

As I grabbed the planchette, the pen fell out, clattered loudly on the floor and rolled under the fridge. I got down on my knees to get it, but Aunt Corinne nervously shouted, "Never mind! Never mind! Just hide *that!*"

I tried to think where to hide the planchette and finally just threw it under the sink. It crashed into some containers. I slammed the cupboard door shut and stood leaning against the counter, trying to look natural. Then I saw the paper. Just as I snatched it off the table and stuffed it under my sweater, the back door burst open. In stepped a chubby red-haired lady in a purple coat. "Merry Christmas, everybody!" She was holding two presents. A big one and a little one.

"Merry Christmas, Ruth." Aunt Corinne gave her a hug. "I thought you were visiting your sister for Christmas."

"Vera caught that darn flu that's goin' 'round," said Ruth. "She catches everything, that one. Includin' a good man. Brazen woman flirted with the doctor and they hooked up! Can you believe it?" She laughed loudly. "This here's your gift, Corinne." She handed over the small box. Great — the big one had to be mine. "And this one's for a little feller named Joey. Have you seen 'im?"

"That's me."

Ruth waddled over but instead of handing me the present, she put it on the table then gave me a bear hug. She lifted me right off the floor. "Merry Christmas, Joey," she said and covered my face with kisses.

"Merry Christmas, Mrs. Simmonds." I could hardly breathe.

"Ah, just call me Ruth. Everybody does."

Ruth put me down and handed over the large present. "Why don't you go put this under the tree? You *do* have a tree, don't you?"

"Actually ..." She could tell I felt a little embarrassed.

"Well, you do now!" She put two fingers in her mouth and out came a loud whistle. The back door opened and in came a Christmas tree with a man at each end.

"Where would ya like it, ma'am?" one of them asked my aunt.

Aunt Corinne's eyes were wide with surprise. "In — in the living room, I guess. Through that door."

She pointed and the tree moved through the kitchen. "What on earth's going on here, Ruth?"

Ruth suddenly got serious. "Everybody should have a Christmas tree. Especially children."

Aunt Corinne smiled and nodded. "I'll dig up some decorations."

"That a girl."

I took my big present and Aunt Corinne's puny one and followed the tree. Ruth settled down on the living room couch, put her feet up and drank two glasses of sherry. "To get the cold outta me bones."

Then she and I started decorating.

It was a great tree. Tall and round and perfect. Not one bald spot. Aunt Corinne barely said a word the whole time. Just sat and watched. I could tell she didn't want company, but I didn't mind. I liked Ruth. She talked a lot and laughed even more. And, she kept telling me really lame jokes and riddles. "Joey, why'd the kid throw butter out the window?"

"I don't know."

"Because he wanted to see butter fly!"

Ruth laughed like crazy, one of those great, jolly laughs. Aunt Corinne didn't laugh once. Not even a smile. I guess Harry was right about the first Christmas being the worst.

Finally, Aunt Corinne went over to the box of decorations and lifted out a sparkly star for the top of the tree. Just as she pulled over a chair to stand on, Ruth jumped up and shouted, "Make a wish! Make a wish!" Her voice was so loud I almost had a heart attack. "Now! Before it's too late!"

We both stared at Ruth like she was out of her mind. She jiggled up and down and pointed at the clock on the mantel. "Look!" she shouted even louder, her finger jabbing the air. "It's 11:11! Do you know how *rare* it is to see 11:11! It's magical! A wish at 11:11 is sure to come true. Hurry. HURRY!"

So many things exploded in my head that I couldn't decide. Then it hit me. I closed my eyes and silently wished that my aunt would be happy again.

When I opened my eyes, I saw Aunt Corinne slowly turn and stare out the living room window at the ocean. What was she waiting for? Ruth looked really anxious. Finally, my aunt whispered, "I wish Stephen had kept his promise."

By the time I could wonder what promise he'd made, the clock changed to 11:12.

"Time's up!" shouted Ruth, slumping into her chair, exhausted. "It's done."

# 14

On Christmas morning I woke up to the sound of birds chirping. In winter? Then I heard something even stranger — my aunt singing. Yup, it was definitely my aunt and she was belting out the second verse of "Joy to the World."

I headed for the kitchen. As I went through the living room, I spotted four presents under the tree and eyeballed the tags — two had my name on them. One was from Ruth, the other from Aunt Corinne. The third present said "Merry Christmas, Mom," which meant Ruth, and the other one said "For Corinne." It was finally starting to feel like Christmas.

When I entered the kitchen, I did a double take. The room was *spotless*. Every square inch. "Wow!"

Aunt Corinne was at the counter, her hands full of dough. She gave me a radiant smile. "Merry Christmas, Joey," she said and kissed me on the forehead.

I couldn't believe it! Her hair was clean and shiny and her eyes twinkled. The dark circles had disappeared and the color was back in her cheeks. "You look beautiful, Aunt Corinne."

"Why, thank you, sir. It's not every day a girl gets a compliment like that."

"What're you making?" I slipped onto the wooden stool to get a better look.

"A Christmas loaf. It's a tradition in these parts."

"I *love* home-baked bread."

"Sorry, honey. This loaf isn't for eating. It's for dividing and scattering to the four corners of the house."

"Dividing and scattering? Why would you want chunks of bread all over the place?"

"For protection, of course." She punched at the dough.

I leaned in. "Protection from *what?*"

"From evil. I don't really believe it, but that's what they say. Maybe when this tradition started, there was more evil around."

Bread protecting you from evil? Action heroes should pack away their guns and start baking Christmas loaf. Bread — a lethal weapon!

"Do you want to help?" my aunt asked. She shook some flour onto a wooden board.

I shrugged. "I guess I should do my part to

fight evil." Aunt Corinne laughed.

I rolled up my pajama sleeves and Aunt Corinne tied an apron around my chest. Don't try to picture it. I looked really dumb. My aunt shook flour over my hands and showed me how to knead the dough. Very cool — you push it and pound it and roll it and moosh it and smoosh it and then squash the sucker with a rolling pin. Bam!

Aunt Corinne was onto "Deck the halls with boughs of holly, Fa la la la la la la la la." On the third verse, a robin landed on the window ledge and looked right at us.

My aunt stopped singing. "Am I imagining things or is that a robin?"

"Looks like a robin to me."

"In *December?*"

We tried to get a closer look but the robin flew away. That's when we saw an even stranger sight — Ruth, jogging toward the house, wearing a bright orange jogging suit. Aunt Corinne wiped her hands and we headed outside.

It was warm. *Really* warm. The fog had lifted and most of the ice had melted. The few icicles still hanging from the roof were dripping. Aunt Corinne looked at the clear blue sky, shielding her eyes from the sun.

"How is this possible?" she asked.

Ruth came around the house, breathing heavily. "Good morning, good morning," she puffed.

"I thought you were still in bed," said my aunt.

"On such a beautiful day?" She sat on the steps to catch her breath. "It's the warmest Christmas I've ever seen. And I've seen plenty of 'em, I can tell you."

Aunt Corinne sat beside Ruth, resting her elbows on her knees. "It feels like those first warm days of spring when everything seems so hopeful."

Ruth nodded. They both looked out over the ocean. Seeing my aunt and Ruth sitting shoulder to shoulder like that made me smile. As I slipped back into the house and headed to my ball of dough, the phone started ringing. I lifted the receiver.

"Hello?"

"Merry Christmas, sweetie!"

"Mom! Merry Christmas!"

"How's everything going? Are you doing okay?"

"I'm doing great. You'll never believe what the weather's —" A loud crackling cut off my last words.

"Didn't hear what you said, Joey."

"The weather! It feels just like summer."

"You're kidding. We're in the middle of an ice storm here."

"Aunt Corinne and I are baking bread." The crackling got even louder.

"What's red?"

"Bread. Bread!"

"Fred?"

The crackling made it impossible to hear. "Sorry, Mom, can't hear you."

Mom mumbled something and then I thought I heard her say, "I'll call back." So I hung up and waited. In less than a minute the phone rang again.

"Mom?"

The sound I heard was like when the cable on your TV suddenly goes down. If she was saying anything, I sure couldn't make it out. I shouted, "If you can hear me, Mom, Merry Christmas! I love you!" Then I hung up. I shrugged and went back to my bread.

A few minutes later, Aunt Corinne and Ruth wandered in.

"Who's the baker?" Ruth asked.

"That would be me," I said, holding up my rolling pin.

"Nice apron." She grinned. "I have one just like it."

Lesson. *Never* let anyone tie an apron on you. You never know who might show up.

While the turkey and Christmas loaf baked, Aunt Corinne and Ruth worked on the rest of the dinner — cranberry sauce, stuffing, mashed potatoes, roasted peppers, peas, cornbread and pumpkin pie. Around one o'clock we sat down to eat. I ate so much I could barely roll myself into the living room and over to the Christmas tree.

Aunt Corinne sat on the floor next to me and Ruth sank into an old green armchair. "Is there anything under that tree for me?" Ruth asked with a twinkle in her eye.

I handed her a present wrapped in shiny red foil. "This is from Aunt Corinne."

Ruth smiled and peeled the bow off the top. Then she stuck it to the side of her head. It looked like something was growing out of her ear. She unwrapped the gift slowly — so slowly you'd think she was doing brain surgery. I wanted to shout "Rip it! Rip it! Just rip the darn thing!"

Ruth must have read my mind. "Half the joy is savoring the moment *before* you open a gift."

I wished she'd savor a little faster.

Ruth crunched the red foil into a tight ball and flung it over her shoulder. It flew clear across the room, bounced off the window and landed in a vase. She held up the gold-colored box and lifted the lid. Inside was white tissue — lots of it. She carefully unwound the tissue and tenderly held up a crystal angel. It was one of the angels I'd seen in Aunt Corinne's room. I guess she hadn't bought a gift for Ruth and had to find something fast.

When the sun hit the angel's wings, it created a rainbow on the wall. Ruth ooohed and ahhhhed. "You know what they say." Her eyes lit up. "Rainbows are answered prayers." She looked directly at Aunt Corinne. "Now I'm *sure* your wish will come true."

Her wish? Then I remembered — she'd wished that Uncle Stephen had kept his promise, whatever it was.

It was my turn. I tore open the present from my aunt in three seconds flat. It was a T38 High-Powered Microscope with nine different lenses. On each lens was a bug ... a dead bug. I tried hard not to let my disappointment show.

"It'll be *great* for school." Aunt Corinne smiled.

"Thanks," I said, with more enthusiasm than I felt. She meant well, but my aunt cared way too much about my mind.

I wanted to grab the big present that Ruth had brought me, but fair is fair. So I reached under the tree and handed Aunt Corinne the tiny gift from Ruth. She did something I never do. She read the card first. "Yesterday is history, tomorrow a mystery, today is a gift. That's why we call it ... the present." My aunt lowered the card and looked at Ruth. Ruth nodded. That look meant something to them but not much to me.

Aunt Corinne unwrapped the little box — a bit faster than Ruth, but still pretty slowly. Inside was a black satin pouch with a silver drawstring. She pulled it open and gently lifted out a gold locket on a chain. As she held the locket up, it spun around, a few turns to the left, then a few to the right. Back and forth it went, like it was dancing.

"It's absolutely lovely, Ruth. Thank you."

My aunt didn't take her eyes off the locket. Neither did I. As it spun back and forth, back and forth I started to feel weird. Sort of like I was about to float away.

"The locket belonged to my mother." Ruth's voice brought me back. "She gave it to me on my twenty-first birthday. Now I want you to have it."

I thought Aunt Corinne was going to bawl, but her eyes just got watery. Thank goodness. I hate when things get mushy. But I love presents. One down, one to go. And it was a big one. I knew I should be polite and wait for Aunt Corinne to put the locket back into the pouch, but I just couldn't. I grabbed Ruth's big gift and ripped off the wrapping paper in one shot. Ruth rubbed her chubby hands together. "I think you're gonna like it."

I pulled the lid off and looked inside. Another box?

"Well, open it," said Ruth, grinning ear to ear.

I lifted out the second box and tore off its wrapping. Inside I found ... another box. "Are you trying to drive me crazy?"

Ruth laughed. "Keep goin', lad. It's worth the work."

I took out the third box, unwrapped and opened it. Yup. *Another* box, but no wrapping this time. Inside was a velvet case. Boy, it sure looked expensive. I flipped open the lid. Then I looked at Ruth and pasted a smile on my face. "*A key?*"

"Yes! Isn't it wonderful?!"

Wonderful? Who was she kidding? A key isn't a gift. At least not where I come from.

"Are you sure you didn't forget something?"

"Like what?" asked Ruth innocently.

"Like something for it to open," I said sarcastically.

"Joey!" Aunt Corinne looked shocked.

"Sorry."

"No, no, no. Joey's right," Ruth said. "What good's a key if it doesn't open something?"

I gave my aunt an "I told you" look.

"Now, let me see." Ruth tapped a finger on her cheek as she looked around the room. "Maybe it opens that drawer," she said, pointing to an antique desk with a lamp on it.

I rushed to the desk and tried to jam the key into the lock. Way too big. "Doesn't fit, Ruth."

"Oh my," she said. "Let me think." If this was some kind of torture it was working. "The jewelry box!" she shouted. "On the mantel next to the clock!"

I raced to the fireplace and inserted the key into the jewelry box. Not even close. "Any other suggestions?" I tried not to sound too annoyed.

Ruth thought for a long time. "Oh yes. *Now* I remember." She slowly raised her hand and pointed to the window that overlooked the cliff. I thought she was pointing at the ocean but then her finger moved to the right and down to an old seaman's chest with iron strips on the lid.

"That chest belonged to Stephen," she said. "His grandfather gave it to him on his tenth birthday. He kept all kinds of toys and things inside."

A *treasure* chest, I thought.

"When he was fifteen," Ruth went on, "Stephen lost the key. He could have pried it open with a crowbar, but he figured he'd find the key eventually. After a while he got too old for the toys inside and ... well, it hasn't been opened in eighteen years."

Now *this* could be interesting. I knelt in front of the chest.

"A while back," said Ruth, "when I was goin' through some of Stephen's old things to give away, I found the darn key inside a shoe. Can you believe it? Eighteen years, sittin' inside an old shoe." She laughed her huge laugh. "Corinne said it was okay with her, Joey, so, whatever's inside, you can have."

My aunt smiled warmly and nodded. I looked at the lock and then at the key and understood what Ruth meant about savoring the moment *before* you open a gift. I took a deep breath and inserted the key into the lock. It slid right in. Half a turn to the right and it clicked open.

# 15

With my hands slightly trembling, I lifted the heavy lid. The hinges made a loud creaking sound. Suddenly, a bright light came shooting out of the chest, almost blinding me. I squinted and saw a flashlight. "This flashlight's still on!" I shouted and grabbed it. "Wait a minute." It didn't make sense. "There's no way a flashlight could stay on for *eighteen* years."

"Maybe the switch hit up against something when you opened the lid," said my aunt.

"Even if it did, the batteries would have corroded ages ago."

"Yes, of course. You're right."

"Now, just a second here," said Ruth. "Seamen's chests had to be sealed tight as a drum to keep everything inside dry in case of a shipwreck. With no air, the batteries would be protected, wouldn't they?"

"Sounds reasonable to me," said my aunt.

Well, it didn't to me. They might be protected from corrosion, but they'd still go dead.

"It's the darnedest thing though," continued

Ruth with a nervous laugh. "When Stephen was little he would always forget to turn off flashlights. No matter how many times his dad and I reminded him, he'd still forget, every single time."

My aunt looked at the flashlight. Her eyes lit up and a huge smile crossed her face. I knew what she was thinking. Uncle Stephen was giving her a sign after all. If she wanted to believe that, it was okay with me.

I flicked the switch to turn off the flashlight. The light stayed on.

"That's funny," I said. "It won't shut off." I tried again. Still nothing. I tilted the flashlight and started to unscrew the base. "I guess I'll have to take out the batteries."

"No!" Ruth and my aunt shouted together. Then they both giggled.

"Please don't take them out, Joey." Ruth sounded desperate.

But it was too late. I'd already looked inside. It was empty. That's when I realized she thought the light was a sign from Uncle Stephen, too. Turning off the light would be like him dying again.

I decided not to tell them that whatever kind of flashlight this was, it didn't run on batteries. I quickly screwed the base back on. "Okay."

I put the flashlight on the carpet. I'd check it out later when they weren't around.

The chest was filled right to the top. What a haul! I grabbed a baseball mitt and a tennis racket and some balls, then lifted out comic books — dozens of them. Superman, the Green Hornet, Spider Man. I reached in again and pulled out two Hardy Boys mysteries and a little leather sack tied with a green string. I quickly undid the string and poured out what was inside. Silver dollars! "This stuff is great!" I glanced over my shoulder at Ruth. "And it's all mine?" She nodded. "Even the money?"

"Whatever's there is yours."

"This is the best Christmas present ever! Thank you!"

There was a metal lantern and a yellow Frisbee, some board games, an old compass and a telescope. Tucked along the side was a jacket like air force pilots used to wear — it fit perfectly.

"You look fabulous!" said Ruth.

"You sure do." Aunt Corinne was smiling.

Something wrapped in a blue blanket was at the bottom of the trunk. I unfolded the blanket and held up what was inside for Ruth and Aunt Corinne to see. "I didn't know Uncle Stephen played the fiddle."

That's when everything changed.

Aunt Corinne stopped smiling. Her eyes got dark, and then a look of anger flashed over her face. She stood up, walked across the room and pushed open the kitchen door. I quickly looked at Ruth. "What's wrong?"

"Nothin' to worry yerself about, Joey." She followed my aunt into the kitchen.

I dropped the fiddle on the couch, moved closer to the door and leaned my ear against it. I heard my aunt say, "Just when the pain was starting to ease a little."

"I'm sorry, Corinne." Ruth's voice was so soft I could barely hear her.

"It's not your *fault,* Ruth. It's nobody's fault." My aunt was shouting. "It's just ..." Then I heard crying. "I should have gone on the boat. I was *meant* to be with him."

"Don't talk like that," pleaded Ruth. "You were saved."

"*Saved?* From what? I'd welcome death — *anything* that'd make me forget!"

"You *want* to *die?!*"

"Yes!" My aunt's voice was hard and cold.

A moment later, the back door slammed.

I started to go into the kitchen when I heard Ruth say, "I know you're lonely. I'm doing *every-*

*thing* I can to help." Who was she talking to? "Be patient — for a little while longer."

Had Aunt Corinne come back? I pushed through the door and saw Ruth sitting at the table. I looked around. No one else was there. "Who are you talking to, Ruth?" She didn't answer. Just got up and walked past me like she didn't even see me. I followed her to the living room. She slowly sat on the couch and stared out the window with a faraway look in her eyes.

"Why did the fiddle upset Aunt Corinne so much?" I asked, almost in a whisper.

Ruth still didn't answer. Finally, she said, "You know your Uncle Stephen drowned, don't ya?"

"Yeah. My mom told me."

Ruth turned to me. "Come here and sit down. I'll tell you exactly what happened."

I sat next to her. Ruth took a long, deep breath then reached inside her blouse and unpinned a small photograph. "This is the last picture taken of Stephen." She handed it to me.

The photograph was of Uncle Stephen standing in front of his boat playing a fiddle, but something looked funny. Then I realized Uncle Stephen was holding the fiddle bow in his left hand.

"Last spring," said Ruth, "your Aunt Corinne and your Uncle Stephen put together all their savings and bought a boat, the kind you take tourists on to show them the sights. Stephen figured he'd take them sightseein' — the cliffs, the lighthouses and, if they were lucky, even some whales. So many visitors come during the summer that I thought it was a grand idea.

"That first trip out, nineteen people paid to go on the tour. The boat had twenty seats, so that left one place — for Corinne. Just as they were headin' out, they heard a voice shoutin' 'Wait for me!' It was a boy about your age, wavin' his arms and tearin' down the hill. He had run all the way from his home at the edge of town. The boy *loved* lighthouses and begged Stephen to let him come. Well, you know yer aunt, she's got a heart a' gold, so she gave up her seat to the lad."

That sounded like something my aunt would do.

"Stephen believed that music made people happy," Ruth continued, "so he brought one of his fiddles along. Just before the boat pulled away, he played a few tunes. That's when Corinne took the picture." I stared at Uncle Stephen's smiling face and could almost hear the music.

"Corinne made him promise to take her with him ... next time. He promised — even crossed his heart and hoped to die."

Now I understood Aunt Corinne's wish.

"A few hours later a storm blew in." A sad look came over Ruth. "Stephen, the boat, all the passengers ... gone."

"They *all* died?"

"Coast guard searched for days. But they never found any debris or ... bodies. What else could have happened?" Ruth gently took the photograph from my hand and held it to her chest. "I can't bear the thought of Stephen being at the bottom of the ocean with only strangers to keep 'im company." Tears rolled down her cheeks. She slowly stood up and walked out of the room.

I sat there alone for a while. I just didn't get it. One minute we were all happy and smiling; the next, everybody was crying. Finally I got up and piled everything back inside the trunk. It all looked like junk now.

I grabbed the fiddle from the couch and set it on top. Then I slammed the lid.

The kitchen door swung open. It was my aunt. She walked over to me, gave me a big hug and apologized for leaving like that. "I really do love having you here, Joey, and I want us both to enjoy our time together. Now, go and get some fresh air while I clean up. It's a beautiful day."

I was glad to get away. Usually when someone apologizes, I can forget about the whole thing. But Aunt Corinne missed Uncle Stephen so much she wanted to die. How do you enjoy your time with someone who'd rather be dead?

# 16

A bird was outside the back door. A dead one. It wasn't on the ground where you'd expect a dead bird to be, but tied with string to the end of a branch. Holding the branch was the same boy who'd waved to me on the hill and at the antique shop.

"Spare a few coins to bury the bird?" he asked. "Mercy to all creatures big and small."

"You want money to bury a *bird?*"

"A nickel, a dime, whatever you can spare."

I fished through my pockets. "All I've got is a quarter and I don't want to part with it."

"For a quarter I'll let you watch. Take you to the secret burial place. No one's ever seen it."

I handed over the quarter.

The boy's name was Tucker and he was a little taller than me. I followed him down a twisty path that led to the bottom of the cliff and then along the rocky shore to a cave. Inside, it was dark and cold. Tucker pulled a flashlight out of his pocket, and the room filled with golden light. Butterflies had been painted all over the cave walls. Hundreds of them.

"Wow! That's unbelievable!"

"Cool, isn't it?" Tucker smiled.

"Who *painted* them?" I walked over to get a better look.

Tucker shrugged. "They were here when I discovered this cave. I asked around but no one knew for sure. A couple of people thought it might be old man Halley."

"Mr. Halley? The guy in the wheelchair?"

"That's him. He's real interested in the Second World War — all those innocent people who got killed. He once told my grandfather that children in concentration camps drew butterflies on the walls. So I figure it's him. Who knows?"

Tucker handed me the branch with the dead bird. "Follow me."

I've always felt creeped out in dark, closed spaces but I really wanted to see this secret burial place. As we moved farther into the cave, it got warmer and warmer — too warm. Finally, we came to a narrow corridor. I followed Tucker through it into another chamber. A nervous, sick feeling bubbled up in the pit of my stomach.

"When the tide comes in, this whole cave fills with water." Tucker's voice bounced off the walls.

I really wish he hadn't said that. When I was five, I went to my friend Jesse Gorden's birthday party. His family had a swimming pool and all the kids jumped off the diving board like it was nothing. Jesse's cousin Crystal teased me because I was afraid, so Jesse said he'd go with me. We climbed up together and edged our way along the board. When I got to the end and looked down, I froze. Then Jesse pushed me.

I didn't have a heart attack or die like I thought I would, just went under the water and came right back up coughing and gasping. Somebody pulled me over to the side and said I'd better stay in the shallow end with the babies. That's a long way of telling you I'm afraid of water.

"How much farther?" I asked.

"Almost there."

At the end of the dark corridor, we crouched down and went through a small opening. "This is it," said Tucker, flashing the light around the walls of a second chamber.

"How'd you ever find this place?"

"One day I was on the shore throwing rocks when this bird flew by and went right into the cave. When I got inside, it was dead. Just like that. Then I saw three other birds lying in the mud. I figured they probably flew in and smacked into the walls."

"So you buried them?"

Tucker looked me straight in the eyes. "Everyone deserves a decent burial."

He handed me the flashlight and knelt down near a row of rocks. Untying the bird, he laid it gently on the floor, then began digging a hole with his hands. He piled the sand to one side. When the hole was pretty deep, he picked up the dead bird, tilted his head upward and closed his eyes. Was he praying? For a bird?

I felt something swirl around my feet. "Tucker, hurry up. Water's coming in!"

Tucker didn't move. It was back — that sick feeling in the pit of my stomach.

More water came in, swishing through the opening. It suddenly looked really small. What if we couldn't crawl back through it? What if the chamber filled up and we drowned? That's when the real panic hit. "Tucker!"

He looked at me with his pale eyes. "It'll only take a minute."

Water was pouring in fast. I could feel my legs shaking. I had to go, *now*. "Stay if you want, but I'm out of here!"

I ran to the opening and bent down low to crawl through. A rush of cold water splashed in, soaking me. I lost my balance and fell. The flashlight slipped out of my hand and washed far back into the cave.

I scrambled up, quickly crawled through the opening and made my way along the dark corridor, pressing my hand against the wall to guide me. The rough stone scraped my palm but I hardly felt it.

The water was nearly up to my knees. As I waded through it, my legs felt like they weighed a ton. The farther I went the more the water seemed to pull me down. I couldn't believe how hard it was to walk through it. Finally, I got to the end of the corridor and entered the first chamber.

Light streamed in. I'd made it!

Outside the cave I gulped the salty air. Fog had rolled in but I could see enough to make my way over the boulders and down to the beach.

I found a big rock and sat down to catch my breath. Everything was calm and quiet. I watched the water roll into the mouth of the cave. It wasn't very high at all. I suddenly felt really stupid. The coward from the city, afraid of a little water.

A beam of light swept across the sand. A few seconds later it swept around again. Then I figured out what it was. The lighthouse beam. I never thought they came on during the day, but I guess sailors can't see in fog either. As the beam went by again, my eye caught something shining near my feet. I bent down and pushed away the sand. It was a watch, one of those old-fashioned ones attached to a chain. The glass covering the face was badly cracked but I held it to my ear anyway. No ticking. I looked at the face again — the watch had stopped at exactly 11:11. I knew my wish probably wouldn't come true but I closed my eyes and shouted, "I wish I was brave!"

The sound of oars cutting through water made me open my eyes. I could barely see through the fog, but when I squinted I could just make out the shape of a small boat ... some kind of rowboat. It pulled up to the shore and a dark figure stepped out onto the beach. Then it turned toward me. I was looking at a skeleton covered in green slime and tattered rags.

And it was looking at me!

# 17

The skeleton quickly moved toward me. I screamed.

"Joey!" Tucker's voice rang out.

The skull snapped in Tucker's direction. Then the skeleton turned and was swallowed up by the fog.

Tucker raced over to me. "What happened?"

I just stood there, staring like a zombie.

"Joey! What's wrong?"

I managed to raise a shaky hand and pointed toward the boat.

Tucker looked over. "The boat?"

I nodded.

"What about it?"

No words came out.

"The boat scared you?"

I nodded again. That's all I could do — nod like some idiot.

"Why did it scare you?" asked Tucker.

Paralyzed with fear, I was unable to utter a sound. With my arm still outstretched, my finger pointing straight ahead, I fainted.

The next thing I knew, Tucker was smacking my face.

"Ow!"

"Joey? Are you okay?"

I remembered the skeleton and sat bolt upright. It had disappeared but the boat was definitely there. I leaped to my feet and ran along the beach to the path that led up to Aunt Corinne's yard.

"Hey! Where are you going?!" shouted Tucker.

"Come on!" I yelled over my shoulder. "Hurry!"

"Why?"

I wasn't hanging around to explain. "We've got to get away from here!"

Tucker just stood there, not moving. Me? I set a new Olympic record scrambling up the side of that cliff. Gasping like crazy, I ran across the yard and burst through Aunt Corinne's door screaming at the top of my lungs. "Aunt Corinne! Ruth! Aunt Corinne!" No one was in the kitchen. "Where are you? Aunt Corinne!" Silence. I ran into the living room. No one was there either. The bedrooms — all empty. "Where *is* everybody?!"

"The fog can play tricks on people." Tucker was standing in my bedroom doorway. "You wouldn't be the first."

"They're gone! He's got them!"

"Got who?" asked Tucker, really calmly.

"Aunt Corinne and Ruth! They've disappeared! He's got them!"

"*Who's* got them?"

"The skeleton!"

Tucker's eyebrows went up. "The *what?*"

"Skeleton! S-k-e-l-e-t-o-n! I saw one step off that boat on the beach!"

"I didn't see any skeleton."

"It disappeared into the fog. You were just coming out of the cave. But it was there! I swear it!"

"Joey, if I were you, I'd keep that to myself."

"Why?!"

In a low voice Tucker said, "Because they'll think you're crazy, then they'll take you away. It happened to a friend of mine, Andy Bursey. He told everybody he saw a spaceship landing in the cemetery — *swore* aliens came out of it. Of course, nobody believed him. Nobody. Not one single person."

"That doesn't mean it wasn't true! Maybe he

*did* see a spaceship and aliens."

"A few days later they found out a blimp had strayed from the mainland. It was advertising space-age shoes." Tucker leaned toward me. "*Shoes.*"

I swallowed hard.

"By the time they told Andy, it was too late. He'd gone nutty for real. He thought he saw something — and he *did*, but it wasn't what he thought. Maybe you did see a skeleton. Or maybe it was something else."

"Like *what?*"

Tucker thought for a second. "Like someone in a costume."

"A *costume!*"

"Actors wear them for movies. And they make movies around here all the time."

"They do?"

"Or maybe it was someone wearing a Halloween costume. I saw a lot of skeleton costumes last Halloween."

Every muscle in my body relaxed. A costume. Of *course*. It was a costume. How could I have been so dumb?

"There's an explanation for everything," said Tucker. "*Everything.*"

"You're probably right, but what *idiot* would be

wearing a Halloween costume at Christmas?"

"That, I don't know. But it happens. People decide to dress funny — whatever."

My body finally stopped shaking. I sat down on my bed feeling a whole lot better. Just like that — one minute I was a raving lunatic and the next I was back to normal. I like it when things make sense, and this explanation did. Someone wearing a costume made a lot more sense than a real skeleton rowing a boat. But I couldn't help wondering — where were Ruth and Aunt Corinne?

"I gotta get goin'," said Tucker.

"You're leaving?"

He smiled. "You'll be all right."

I followed him to the back door and waved good-bye. There was something about Tucker that I really liked.

As I closed the door, a car pulled up. I went outside and saw Aunt Corinne and Ruth getting out of Ruth's car. I looked around for Tucker but he was nowhere in sight. How could he have got down the hill so fast?

Aunt Corinne picked up two brown bags.

"Where'd you go?" I sounded mad.

"Didn't you see my note?"

"What note?"

"Right there on the kitchen table," said Ruth. "We went to my house." She lifted a large box out of the trunk.

"Sorry if we worried you, honey," said my aunt. "But we couldn't find you."

"I was helping to bury a bird."

"That's nice," she smiled, as though burying birds was a regular thing to do. Maybe in Monk's Cove it was.

In the house, Ruth carefully set her box on the kitchen table, then lifted the lid and took out a goldfish bowl. "This is Charlie," she said. "Didn't want 'im to starve, so I thought I'd bring 'im along. He doesn't get out much these days." She laughed and handed me the bowl. "Find a nice spot for 'im, will ya? That's a good lad."

As I took Charlie, I glanced into the box filled with food. "We needed to pick up some goodies," Ruth said with a grin as she started to pull things out. "Cheese and crackers, moose burgers, bickies, a Christmas log cake and ..." She lifted a huge bottle, "... my famous dogberry wine."

"We having a party?"

"Maybe ... maybe not," she said mysteriously, winking at me.

I carried Charlie into the living room and

put him on a table beside the door. There was a plant on the table, too — something for Charlie to look at.

The morning after Christmas, snow covered everything like a big white blanket. Tucker was walking up the hill toward the house holding another branch, with another dead bird on it. Where was he finding them?

I jumped into my clothes, pulled on my boots and raced outside. No Tucker. Where could he have gone? I followed his footprints through the yard, my feet sinking into the soft snow. At the edge of the cliff, I looked down. Not there either. Unless Tucker could fly, there's no way he could have made it down to the beach. It didn't make sense — and I hate it when things don't make sense.

I slowly headed back. The snow felt really soft under my feet, almost too soft for snow. And it was so bright. I don't remember ever seeing snow this bright before. It almost blinded me. With each step, all I thought of was Tucker. I *know* I saw him coming up the hill.

The back steps creaked under my feet. As I stepped into the porch, I heard them creak again.

# 18

Spinning around, I saw Tucker and gasped.

"You're not going to faint again, are you?" he asked.

"Where'd you come from?"

"Home, of course." He grasped the doorknob.

I'm not sure why, but I yanked the door out of his hand and slammed it shut. Then I locked it.

"Hey!" yelled Tucker. "What'd you do that for?"

"I ... I don't know."

"Well, open up."

"No."

"What d'ya mean, no? What's got into you?"

"I saw you coming up the hill, Tucker. I *know* I saw you. And then you disappeared. Into thin air. Explain *that*."

Tucker looked at me like I was crazy. "I didn't disappear. A cat came out of nowhere, grabbed my sparrow and ran under your house. I went after it."

"You've been under the house?"

Tucker nodded. "At the side, where the wood's fallen away. I didn't get very far, though. I'm too big."

That made sense. I felt better and reached up to unlock the door. Suddenly, I stopped.

"Now what?" Tucker was starting to sound frustrated.

"How do you explain the footprints?"

"*What* footprints?"

I pointed to the snow-covered yard behind the house. "Those footprints," I said. "They're fresh. They go right to the edge of the cliff."

"I don't know anything about those footprints." He sounded angry. Then his voice softened. "Why don't we go check them out?"

Something told me I was safer inside, but my imagination gets carried away sometimes. It's from watching too many scary movies on TV, Aunt Corinne would say.

"Come on, Joey. What are you afraid of?"

I wasn't quite sure. Tucker seemed pretty normal, except for the dead bird stuff. What's the worst he could do? Push me over the cliff? Oh great.

"There's an explanation for everything," he said.

I nodded, unlocked the door and stepped outside.

When Tucker got to the footprints, he bent down and examined them. Then he stood and walked beside them right to the edge of the cliff.

"Well," I said, "what's the explanation?"

"Don't rush me." Tucker bent down again.

"Why would anybody walk through our yard to go down the cliff?" I asked.

Tucker stood up. "They didn't. These footprints head *away* from the cliff. Someone came up from the beach, walked through your yard, then headed down the hill."

"What?"

"Look for yourself. The larger part of each print faces away from the cliff. The heel is at the back. Whoever it was," he pointed toward town, "went that way."

Tucker was right. The footprints headed away from the cliff. "And another thing," he said. "These prints are smooth." He lifted his right foot and showed me the bottom of his boot. "My boots are ridged."

"So whose prints are they?"

Tucker raised both arms like a zombie. "The skeleton," he said in a spooky voice. Then he laughed. So did I.

"Do you want to come tobogganing? Lots of kids are already out."

"Sure. But I have to tell my aunt. Come inside."

"Um. I'll wait for you here, okay?"

"Okay."

In the living room, Ruth was in her bathrobe sprinkling fish food over Charlie's bowl.

"Ruth, when Aunt Corinne wakes up, would you tell her I've gone tobogganing?"

"You be careful, eh?"

"I will."

Tucker and I headed down the snow-covered hill toward town. The weather was so mild that neither of us wore a coat. As we walked along, I told Tucker about Ruth saying there *might* be a party tonight. Or there might not. "Just in case, she brought lots of food from her house. I'm confused."

"She's preparing for the mummers."

"Mummers?"

"They'll probably come because everyone knows your aunt's moving away. This will be her last Christmas here."

"*Who'll* come?"

"The mummers."

"Let's start over. What's a mummer?"

Tucker bent down, scooped up some snow and patted it into a firm ball. "Mummers are just people — friends and neighbors, usually — who show up at your house the night after Christmas. They wear costumes made from whatever bits and pieces are lying around."

"So it's a costume party?"

"Sort of. But only the mummers wear them. And not just over their bodies. Their heads are covered, too."

"How come?"

"So no one will know who they are, of course."

"Why the mystery?"

"That's part of the fun." Tucker threw the snowball. "Mummers bring instruments — accordions, banjos, whatever. They play music and everybody dances and has a good time."

"Do you ever find out who they are?"

"Sometimes. You can guess as much as you like. If you're right, the mummers have to show their faces. It's called 'the unveiling.' If nobody guesses, they leave without anyone knowing who they are and move on to the next house."

I'd never heard of anything like this before. I could hardly wait for night to fall.

I was thinking so hard about mummers that we got all the way up the tobogganing hill before I realized we were in a cemetery. Just past the tombstones was a steep drop-off. "What are we doing here?"

"Best hill in town," said Tucker. "It's a *great* ride."

"Where are the other kids?"

"They're on the bunny hill. This is Dead Man's Hill. Parents don't let their kids come up here. Too dangerous."

"Then why are *we* here?"

"Because it'll be fun."

I leaned over the edge. "Your mother lets you toboggan down *this?*"

"My mother's dead," said Tucker, just like somebody would say *Pass me a sandwich*. "She plugged a toaster into an outlet."

"How can somebody die from plugging in a toaster?"

"The cord was frayed." He brushed some snow off the top of a tombstone. "Our dog spilled his water bowl and what with the water under my mom's feet, electricity shot through her. I was wearing rubber-soled running shoes or it would have fried me too."

"Gee, I'm sorry, Tucker."

"Don't be," he said. "It's the past. I live in the present."

This was an odd place for someone who lives in the present.

"I love graveyards." It was as though Tucker had read my mind. "So many beautiful head-stones. Wanna see my favorite?"

"Yeah, I guess."

"It's over there." Tucker headed toward some newer stones.

As we walked, our feet sank into the deep white snow. It seemed even brighter here — it actually sparkled, like millions of diamonds. Tucker stopped at a large headstone with a white marble angel on top. Under the angel it said, *And upon the farthest shore lands the voyager at last.* Then there was a whole list of names. "How can this many people be buried in one place?"

"They aren't. This stone is in memory of them," said Tucker.

"Where are the bodies?"

"Rotting away at the bottom of the ocean."

"You mean ... these are the people who were on the boat with my uncle?"

Tucker nodded.

I started reading the chiseled names ... Sarah Marie Little, James Grey, Daniel S. Lambert, Lisa Mercer. A shiver ran through me. By the time I got to my uncle's name — Stephen Elijah Simmonds — I felt like crying.

"So many people," said Tucker. "Alive one minute. Dead the next."

Just like the birds. Soaring through the air one minute, dead in the cave the next.

Tucker knelt in front of the stone and ran his finger down the names. He stopped near the bottom of the list. "This was my best friend, David T. Lindley."

"Your mom *and* your best friend are both dead?"

"Like I said, it's the past." Tucker walked away. "Let's go for a ride."

I looked at my uncle's name and quietly whispered, "Good-bye — I wish I'd known you." Then I followed Tucker to the edge of the hill.

I took another look at the slope. It was really steep and there were trees everywhere. "Well," I said, "my mother's still alive and there's no way she'd let me go down *that*."

Tucker ducked in behind some bushes and came out carrying a large piece of cardboard. "What mothers don't know can't hurt them."

"*That's* your toboggan?"

Tucker lined up the cardboard, sat down on it and dug his heels into the snow. "Hop on."

"Are you *crazy?* This hill's way too steep."

"I go down all the time. Broke a collarbone once, but that's because I was showing off."

I felt torn. If I didn't go, I'd feel like a real wuss. Tucker had already seen me faint *and* act like a jerk about the stupid footprints. I hated to sound like a coward, especially since he was so confident. On the other hand, if I went down Dead Man's Hill and broke my neck, then where'd I be? In the morgue. That's where.

"I'm not going, Tucker."

"You're chickening out?"

"I'm no chicken. But I'm not stupid either. We could get killed. Look at all those trees."

Tucker stared at me for a long moment. "A coward dies a thousand deaths, a hero dies but once."

With that, he pushed off, soaring down the hill, maneuvering the cardboard left and right, not going anywhere near the trees. When he reached the bottom he slid and cheered. Before he could look up at me, I hid behind a gravestone. I didn't want to give him the satisfaction of knowing that I'd watched.

I felt like such a loser. If I had just gone down that hill! Would have had the ride of my life. When the going gets tough, I cave. That's the truth of it.

When I got back to the house, Tucker was sitting on the porch steps. "How'd you get here before me?"

"You missed a great ride, Joey."

I sat down beside him. "Don't rub it in."

"You didn't think it was safe and you didn't go. No big deal."

"What about a coward dying a thousand deaths?"

"It's true. What can I say?"

Tucker got up and walked over to a patch of snow. The sun had melted most of it but there were still a few patches left. He packed some snowballs and began throwing them over the cliff. I threw a couple, too. His went farther, of course.

As I started to throw another snowball, I suddenly saw something that made me think I was dreaming. An iceberg was slowly sailing by. It was the freakiest, most beautiful thing I'd ever seen. With my eyes glued to that incredible sight, I felt a soft breeze on my face, but it was like my body had melted away.

"I should warn you." Tucker's voice brought me back with a jolt. "Some mummers've been known to steal things during a party. So make sure your aunt puts her stuff in a safe place — money, jewelry, whatever."

"Don't you *see* it?" I said, pointing to the iceberg.

Tucker looked over. "Sure." He threw another snowball.

"*Sure?* That's all you've got to say?"

"What do you want me to say?"

"An iceberg the size of a football stadium floats by and you've got nothing to say?!"

Tucker looked at it again. "It's big."

"*Big?*"

"I was really impressed the first time I saw one, too," he said. "But we get them a lot around here."

"You're kidding!"

"Nope. Every spring they show up." I shook my head in disbelief. "Although," Tucker went on, "this is the first one I've seen in winter." He let another snowball fly. It soared, arced and then fell into the ocean. "Like I was saying. Tonight, when the mummers come? Nothing's safe. So keep your eyes open."

"But I don't want to miss the party ... if there's even going to be one."

"I'll tell you what. For a few measly dollars, I'll be your security guard."

"How many measly dollars?"

"Three. And that's a darn good deal."

"You're on."

We heard a sound and suddenly the big gray cat came out from under a blue plastic sheet covering a pile of wood. My body tensed up as it rubbed up against my legs.

"That's the cat that took my bird," said Tucker.

As he reached to pat it, I yelled, "Don't! He's dangerous!"

Tucker looked at the cat. It meowed sweetly and plunked itself right on my feet. "*This* cat?" asked Tucker, stroking its big ugly head. The cat purred.

Of course it was *this* cat, but you'd never know it. How could he have changed so much? The darn thing even rolled over on its back so Tucker could scratch its belly. "Go ahead. Make a liar out of me."

After a few minutes, Tucker headed home.

"What about the party?" I asked.

"I'll be back," he said, "after dark." And he was gone.

We stood there, me and the cat, staring out over the cliff at the iceberg. It started raining. Soft, gentle rain. Then, from out of nowhere, a rainbow appeared. Answered prayer, Ruth had said. Answered prayer.

# 19

By dark, the rain was really pouring down, but that didn't stop people from coming over. Harry and Maxine were the first to arrive. Then about ten of Aunt Corinne's and Ruth's friends showed up one after the other. Everyone had the same idea about the mummers visiting because of Aunt Corinne leaving and all. I hoped they were right.

I kept a lookout for Tucker. Where was he? Maybe the rain was keeping him away. Maybe his dad wouldn't let him come.

Finally, just before eight, he showed up. While the grown-ups talked in the living room, Tucker and I went to my bedroom, turned out the lights and pulled chairs over to the window. We had a great view of the hill leading up to the house.

An hour later we were still sitting there. "Do you think they'll come, Tucker?"

"I told you. No one knows for sure."

"But do you *think* they'll come?"

"Yeah, I do."

"Even in this lousy weather?"

"Newfoundlanders never let a little rain stop them. Besides, mummers go to more than one house in a night. This one's the farthest out. They'll get here, eventually."

By ten o'clock my confidence in the mummers coming to our house was totally gone. I was bored stiff. "You might as well go home, Tucker," I said, stifling a yawn. "It's not going to happen."

At that exact moment, a loud knock shook the window. Our heads snapped in the direction of the sound. Tucker smiled. I didn't. Staring at us was something — someone — with its head wrapped in a burlap bag tied at the throat with rope. Two holes were cut out for the eyes, but all you could see was blackness. My stomach tightened.

"They're here!" shouted Tucker, bolting out of the room.

I just stared — and the mummer stared back. Then he lifted his hand and gave me a little wave.

"Oooh, that's a scary one," said Aunt Corinne, coming up behind me. She waved back at the mummer.

We went to the kitchen, where people had gathered, and stood watching as two other mummers came in. They shook the rain off. "Come in. Come in," said Aunt Corinne. She seemed happy to see them.

"Off with yer muddy boots, the both of ya," ordered Ruth.

"No, no, no. It's all right," said my aunt.

"Nonsense," insisted Ruth. "Everyone else 'as and they can, too."

As the two mummers removed their boots, I noticed that one was holding a small accordion and the other a guitar. It was kind of small, too. The mummer with the guitar was dressed in what looked like Salvation Army rejects — large trousers and a mismatched shirt. He had a white veil over his face that was kept in place by a woolen hat. The other mummer had a clown's head and a straw hat. He wore a large, ratty bathrobe with a lady's brassiere over it. My eyes opened wide. Ha! Jack from the antique shop! Jack knew I knew it was him and held a finger up to his lips. "Shhhh."

He grabbed Ruth and danced her into the living room. Everybody laughed and followed. Everybody but me.

I waited for the last mummer, the one in the burlap bag. Finally, he came in, wearing a long black coat that went all the way to his feet. He slowly removed his black rubber boots. Why wasn't he holding any instrument? As he passed me, I felt a chill, like the temperature had suddenly dropped.

In the living room, everybody was ready for a party. The mummer with the veil over his face sat down on Maxine's lap and gave her a big hug.

"Give us a kiss," said Maxine and started to lift his veil. The mummer pulled away, shaking his finger at her. Everybody laughed again.

The clown mummer unlatched the leather strap on his accordion and started playing a lively tune. The other mummer started doing a dance and people stamped their feet to the music.

From my spot near the fireplace, I noticed the third mummer standing next to the Christmas tree, watching through those black holes.

The mummer wearing the veil stopped dancing, picked up his guitar and started playing. People began dancing. The party had *finally* begun.

At the end of the tune, everybody clapped and cheered. Ruth took out her handkerchief and mopped her forehead. "Haven't danced in years. Forgotten how much fun it could be."

Her partner, Dr. Gibbons, a round, curly-haired man with a large bushy mustache said, "I'll go get us something cold to drink, Ruth." Then he gave her hand a squeeze. Ruth blushed.

I looked around for Tucker and spotted him walking into the kitchen. I headed over, and just as I was about to go through the door, it swung open. Aunt Corinne came out carrying a tray of food.

"Did you meet my friend Tucker?" I asked.

"Who's Tucker?"

"He just went in the kitchen."

"Nobody's in there, honey."

"But ..."

"This food's getting cold, Joey. Would you mind clearing some space for it?"

As I cleared away the dishes, a lady named Lydia told Dr. Gibbons that she'd seen a bee that afternoon. "And the darn thing had the nerve to *sting* me! Right on me arse!"

"A *bee?* In December?" Dr. Gibbons shook his head. "Something strange is definitely going on with this weather."

Tucker came over to the table.

"Hey, Tucker. I want you to meet my aunt."

"I already met her. In the kitchen."

I frowned and looked at Aunt Corinne. She was talking with some ladies.

Just then the two mummers took a break and came over to the food table. A man standing nearby squeezed the arm of the mummer with the clown's head. "Too muscular to be a woman," he said. Another man added, "That must be yur mudder's bra."

The mummer with the veil loaded some food onto a plate. As he reached across the table for a glass, Dr. Gibbons grinned. "You're Aidan O'Brien! Yes, you are. Aidan O'Brien!"

Everyone stopped to see if there would be an unveiling. The mummer looked at Dr. Gibbons for a long moment. Then he put down his plate and slowly lifted his veil. "You're right, doc!" Everybody clapped. Aidan shook his head. "No one has *ever* guessed that quickly. What gave me away?"

"Why, that scar on your thumb!" said Dr. Gibbons, smiling ear to ear. "You were born with two thumbs. I removed the extra one when you were a year old. I'd recognize my handiwork anywhere!"

"Next time I'll wear mitts," said Aidan and then he laughed.

I looked at Jack, the mummer with the clown's head. He had bare hands, too. When I glanced at the tree, the third mummer had moved. He was sitting on Uncle Stephen's wooden chest. And he was wearing gloves.

The music started up again, with Jack playing his accordion. People joined in, singing and clapping. At the end of the song a skinny man named Jerrod suddenly called out, "You're Jim St. Croix! You're my cousin, Jim. Right?"

We all looked at Jerrod and the mummer. The clown face shook his head, no.

"Are you sure?" asked Jerrod. "You smell like Old Spice cologne and Jim practically bathes in it."

Again the mummer shook his head and moved away. When he passed a rosy-cheeked lady named Donna, she said, "Would you happen to be Jim's *brother*, Jack?"

The mummer stopped cold. She was right! "Yes!" he bellowed, pulling off his straw hat and clown mask. Donna squealed with delight. Everybody clapped again.

"What made you guess Jack?" asked Ruth.

"Well," Donna said, grinning, "I figured he might be trying to make people *think* he was Jim by putting on his cologne. To throw us off the scent!"

Everyone laughed at her joke. I didn't get it at first but then I clued in — Cologne? Scent? Get it? Really lame, but funny, sort of.

"That's *exactly* what I did." Jack laughed as he swung Donna around. She shrieked like a little girl.

"And then there was one," said Dr. Gibbons ominously.

All eyes went to the mummer sitting on the chest.

## 20

"I'm dedicating this song to you, Donna." Jack smiled and started playing. Everyone gathered around and began clapping to the beat.

The mysterious mummer stood up and lifted the lid of the chest. The light from the flashlight shone on him as he took out Uncle Stephen's fiddle. How did he know there was a fiddle inside? Aunt Corinne was frowning. "Just what does he think he's doing?" She sounded really mad.

The mummer tuned the fiddle, carried it to the Christmas tree, tucked it under his chin and started playing. Boy, was he good! Then it hit me. He was playing left-handed, just like Uncle Stephen.

"I don't want him touching Stephen's fiddle," said Aunt Corinne through clenched teeth.

"Let him be." Ruth's voice was gentle. "He isn't hurtin' anyone."

"He's hurting *me*," said Aunt Corinne.

"Don't go embarrassin' yerself and everyone else." Ruth's voice turned really firm. "It's just a darn fiddle, for heaven's sake."

No one noticed the first mummer, Aidan, walk out of the living room. No one, except Tucker. He caught my eye and motioned for me to follow. When we got to the hallway, I asked, "What's up?"

Tucker put his finger to his lips and pointed to my room. We tiptoed to the door. When we peeked through the crack, we spotted Aidan standing by the dresser holding my Game Boy. Tucker and I pushed the door completely open.

"What are you doing in here?" I asked.

Aidan was so surprised he dropped the Game Boy on the floor. "You scared the heck out of me. Didn't anybody teach you to knock?"

"This is *my* room," I said. "I don't *have* to knock."

"You've got a point there," he laughed. "I'm the one who shoulda knocked." He picked up the Game Boy and put it back on the dresser. "Sorry. Ruth told me the bathroom was this way. I guess I took a wrong turn."

"It's next door," I said.

"Next door. Right."

Aidan walked past us, whistling along with the fiddle.

"Do you believe him?" Tucker asked after Aidan had left.

"The bathroom *is* next door," I said. "It could have been an honest mistake."

I tucked my Game Boy into the dresser drawer. As I closed the drawer the piece of paper that had been under the planchette got stuck. I pulled it out to show Tucker. Suddenly I saw it reflected in the mirror. The words, seen backward, read:

*umbra mortis*

I recognized "umbra." That was one of the words scratched into the cabinet in the antique shop. It was Latin. What did Jack say it meant? Shadow! That was it. Shadow of a smile! But what was "mortis."

"Tucker?"

"Yeah?"

"Do you know what the word 'mortis' means? It's Latin."

"Sure. When I was an altar boy, I heard it all the time at funerals. It means death."

"Death!"

"Why are you asking?"

"The shadow of death *comes!* That's what the voice said."

"What voice?"

"But why would the planchette *write* it when Aunt Corinne asked Uncle Stephen to speak to her? Maybe the warning wasn't for Mr. Halley! Maybe Mr. Halley's brother was warning my *aunt!*"

"Earth to Joey."

"Look, Tucker!" I held the paper up close to the mirror. "See — 'umbra mortis'! Shadow of death!"

Tucker squinted at the mirror. "Looks like gobbledygook to me."

Was I losing my mind? I was starting to sound like a lunatic again. Just like Andy Bursey. And look what happened to him. Straight to the nuthouse. I forced myself to calm down. Be rational. It's just gobbledygook. Don't say another word.

Tucker glanced around the room. "Looks like he didn't touch anything else. But I'll stay here for a while — watch who comes and goes."

"But what about *umbra mortis?*" I just couldn't let it go.

"What about it?" asked Tucker, sounding irritated. "It's just words."

"But it means —"

"I know, I know. Shadow of death. What do

you wanna do? Stop the party and make an announcement?"

Tucker was right. What could anybody do about a couple of Latin words on a piece of paper? I stuffed it back in the drawer.

Tucker smiled. "Now, go have a good time."

"Okay." I walked slowly over to the door. "But if somebody figures out who that third mummer is, you're gonna miss the unveiling."

"Duty first," said Tucker and saluted.

When I got back to the living room, everybody was listening to the mummer wearing the burlap bag. I leaned against the doorframe and thought about the words on the paper. Shadow of death. It had to mean something. But what? When the song ended someone shouted, "Yer Tom Jenkins, Henry's boy, ain'cha! He's left-handed."

I held my breath. Were we finally going to see the fiddler's face? The mummer shook his head, no. Darn. Then he raised the fiddle to his chin again and started playing. The song was so sweet and sad that some people started crying. Ruth leaned into Aunt Corinne. "He plays beautifully, doesn't he?"

Aunt Corinne nodded. "That he does."

I saw her wipe a tear. All her anger seemed to have melted away.

The living room felt really cold. I looked over and saw that the fire had gone out. Just then Aidan walked by and whispered, "It's freezing in here. Let's you and me go get more firewood."

I followed him into the kitchen and over to the back door. He slipped on his work boots, then went outside. So many shoes and boots were piled on top of one another that I couldn't even see mine. I finally just grabbed the nearest pair, the last mummer's black rubber boots. They were big and my feet slipped in easily, but something felt strange. Inside, the boots were ... slippery — sort of slimy.

"Come on!" shouted Aidan, lifting the blue plastic sheet off the wood. I walked over to him and he loaded me up with three big chunks. "That'll do it," he said. "It's so warm out we should just open a window." He was right. The rain had stopped and the air was really warm. Why did the house feel so cold inside?

As we walked back, I asked Aidan if he could give me a hint about who the third mummer was?

"Oh, I couldn't do that now." He laughed.

"I swear I won't tell."

Aidan smiled. "To tell ya the truth, I haven't the foggiest. He joined me and Jack as we was comin' up the hill."

Aidan opened the door. We heard loud music — a lively foot-stomping fiddle tune. The door to the living room opened and Ruth came through wearing big old running shoes. They looked funny with her dress.

"Ah, there you are, Joey," she said, fanning herself with a hankie as she headed out the door. "I'm just goin' for a breath of fresh air."

My arms were full and there was no place to set down the wood, so I wiped my feet and used my back to push open the door to the living room. That's when I caught Aidan reaching for the Christmas loaf on the windowsill.

"Don't!"

Aidan froze.

"That's a Christmas loaf, for dividing and scattering."

"Dividin' and scatterin'?" He laughed. "Don't tell me ya believe all that stuff about protection?"

"Not really, but you still *can't* eat it. There's lots of food in the living room. Please leave that alone."

"All right ... all right," he said, raising his

hands in surrender. Then he sat down and took off his boots.

In the living room the music was even louder. Everybody was pounding their feet and making a terrible racket. Before I reached the fireplace, Dr. Gibbons twirled around and banged into me, hard. The logs went flying — landing right on the food table! I closed my eyes and waited for someone to yell at me but everybody just kept dancing.

That's when I noticed the strange look on their faces. Scared. They looked really scared.

The music got louder still, and people started banging into things. What was going on?

As soon as Aidan came in, he began dancing and stamping his feet, too. A vase on the mantel smashed to the floor. No one even noticed.

"Stop!"

Everyone kept dancing.

"Stop!" I shouted really loudly.

But they didn't stop. Not one of them. They just kept dancing and the mummer kept fiddling.

I looked around and spotted Harry. "Please stop, Harry!" I yelled right in his ear, but he kept dancing like he didn't hear me.

I raced over to Aunt Corinne and grabbed

her. A strong jolt of electricity shot up my arm. I yelled out and pulled away.

"Aunt Corinne! What's going on?!"

My aunt looked like she was about to cry but she kept dancing, too.

Really high-pitched sounds filled the air and the floor suddenly felt funny — wobbly, like at the fun house. I could hear wood cracking. Then I remembered — the foundation had rotted! If people kept pounding, the beams would break and the whole house would go crashing down the cliff!

A low rumbling came from the walls. Then it was like an earthquake hit. Dishes and glasses crashed to the floor. Paintings flew off the wall. The fish bowl slid across the table and got wedged against the plant.

People started crying and screaming. But no one stopped dancing. Through all the screaming, I heard the mummer shout, "I'm keeping my promise, Corinne! This time I'll take you with me!"

# 21

Uncle Stephen? How could it be Uncle Stephen? He was *dead!* I ran up to the mummer, and yanked off the burlap mask. Underneath was a skull! The nose and eye sockets were big black holes, and decaying teeth grinned in the jaw. The mouth hissed, "It's too late!"

I stood, frozen in terror.

"I've come back for you, Corinne!" the mummer shouted again.

"This *can't* be happening!" I had to be dreaming. But why couldn't I wake up?

I looked around. The dancers' eyes were blazing with fear. It was as though a spell had been cast and no one could control what they were doing. That's when the thought hit me. Why wasn't I dancing? Why wasn't the music affecting me?

As I staggered around trying to understand the madness, my eye saw something at the window. Ruth! She was outside staring in. She looked scared.

"Ruth!" I shouted. "Help!"

Jack banged into me, his foot smashing down on my toe. I stumbled back onto the couch and pulled my foot out of the boot. When I put my heel on the floor a *huge* charge of electricity shot up my leg. I screamed and lifted my foot, but quickly realized it didn't hurt. The electricity wasn't a shock. It was more like an energy. I looked at my other foot still in the boot. Was *that* it? Was the rubber protecting me the way rubber soles had protected Tucker when his mom put the plug in the socket?

I grabbed the boot that had fallen, pulled it on and cautiously stepped on the floor again. Nothing. Nothing at all. I *was* protected!

Protection — that made me remember the Christmas loaf. I had to scatter the loaf to the four corners, like Aunt Corinne said.

I raced across the room and bolted through the door. The kitchen *wasn't* shaking. It was perfectly still. I grabbed the loaf from the windowsill, dug my fingers into it and pulled out four clumps. Then I ran back to the living room.

Trying to keep my balance, I made my way to the first two corners of the shaking room, dropping one piece of bread in each and shouting, "Please protect us! Please protect us!"

As I headed for the third corner, the floor-board beneath my feet cracked. I froze and looked around. Ruth was still watching through the window. I pounded on the pane. "Help, Ruth! Help me!"

Ruth turned away from the window. Finally, she was coming to help. Thank you, thank you. I made my way to the third corner and dropped the bread. "Please protect us!" I prayed.

I maneuvered my way through the dancing bodies to the last corner near the fireplace. As I dropped the bread, Tucker caught it and popped it into his mouth.

"No, Tucker! Noooo!"

"I can't let you do that, Joey," he said in a really calm voice. And then an evil smile crossed his face.

"Tucker?"

"The name is David ... David T-for-Tucker Lindley. You remember, don't you? I showed you my name on the tombstone."

A new wave of fear flooded my body. "How can you be David? David's *dead!*"

"Are you sure?" asked Tucker, smiling sweetly.

"Yes!" I screamed. "I'm *sure!*" I raced to get more bread.

When I reached the kitchen door, Tucker was blocking my way. He couldn't possibly have got there that fast!

"Are you sure?" he asked again.

"Come with me, Corinne!" shouted the skeleton. "I'll take you with me! Just like I promised! Just like you wished!"

That's exactly what Aunt Corinne *had* wished for at 11:11 on Christmas Eve. *She* brought him back!

"Be careful what you wish for, eh, Joey?" Tucker was reading my mind.

"She's not going with him!" I tried to push my way into the kitchen. I had to get the bread!

Tucker grabbed me, lifted me right off the floor and flung me across the room like a rag doll. I crashed onto the stone ledge around the fireplace, my hands smashing into the hot coals. Crying out, I jerked my hands away.

Tucker, hovering above the floor, walked over and sat in a chair as if nothing was happening. "Stephen's lonely at the bottom of the ocean," he said. "Your aunt will keep him company. It's what they both want. It's the right thing."

"The right thing?!" I shouted over the music. "Why should she *die?*"

"She was meant to be on that boat, not me. It's her fault I died."

"She was being nice to you! She didn't have to give up her seat. She was being *nice!*"

"Joey!" It was Ruth.

"Ruth! You've got to help me!"

"Come with me. There's still time," she said.

"No! We've got to do something!"

"There's nothing we can do! Come on! Hurry!"

"What about Aunt Corinne and everybody?"

"It's too *late* for them! I'm sorry."

"It's not too late! Ruth! Please!"

"Corinne made her wish, Joey. I didn't know it would turn out like this, but it's *too late* now! There's no going back!"

"What are you talking about?"

"It's what she wanted! *Exactly* what she wanted!"

"She doesn't want to die! Not really!"

Ruth got a strange look in her eyes. "And Stephen won't be lonely anymore."

"Are you crazy?!"

Ruth's face hardened.

"Crazy?" said Tucker. "She's brilliant. The way

she tricked your aunt into making that wish was pure genius. And that wish is going to make everything right. Your aunt will take my place at the bottom of the ocean. She and Stephen are meant to be together."

"No!"

The room tilted. Ruth almost lost her balance. I hung on to the bricks of the fireplace so my body wouldn't touch the floor. As I anxiously looked around at all the people, a chill went up my spine. "Everybody's going to die. In order to get Aunt Corinne, they're *all* going to die!"

"This isn't the way I wanted it to turn out," said Ruth. "But there's nothing I can do about it. They're in the wrong place at the wrong time. Just like that young lad on the boat."

"That's me." Tucker smiled.

"But it'll be over soon," Ruth continued. Then she grabbed my arm. I pulled away hard and screamed. "NO! I'm not leaving Aunt Corinne!"

"If that's the way you want it," said Ruth. Then with one quick movement, she reached down and yanked my boots off. "Goodbye, Joey." She turned and made her way through the dancing bodies.

"Ruth!" She didn't look back. "Ruth!!"

Tucker crossed his arms. "Why don't you join the dance?" he said, with a huge grin on his face. "It's not like you're getting out alive."

Just as Ruth pushed open the kitchen door, a terrifying screech cut through the air. She screamed then jumped back. Something had leaped on her. It was the cat!

Ruth stumbled and fell against the table. The fishbowl crashed to the floor. Then Ruth fell right on top of it, her hands sliding through the water and shattered glass. I looked on in horror as fireworks of blue electrical currents streaked through her body. Within seconds she was dead. So was the cat.

"Too bad," said Tucker unemotionally.

Just then the last lamp fell over. As the bulb smashed against the floor, the room plunged into darkness. I noticed a glow coming from the chest. It shone toward the big living room window and I could see the edge of the cliff. It was right there. We were going to crash down the side any second!

The clock had fallen off the mantel and was dangling by its cord. In the dark room, the digital numbers shone bright red. It was 11:10. Any second now ... any second ... please ...

please. Then — yes! 11:11. I yelled, "Tucker! Uncle Stephen! I wish you'd go back where you came from!"

With a loud cracking of the foundation beams, the floor split and a strong wind rose up out of the earth.

Tucker shrieked, "What have you done?!" Then, right in front of my eyes, he transformed into a skeleton and lunged at me.

With all my might, I kicked out with both feet, catching him in the chest. He reeled backward, crashing into the mummer. The house gave a violent jerk, sending Tucker and the mummer crashing through the window. They fell silently, so silently, down the side of the cliff ... disappearing into the blackness.

I slowly got up. Aunt Corinne's eyes met mine. "You saw it, didn't you, Aunt Corinne?" She nodded, then came over and wrapped her arms around me. As we held each other, everyone else got up, looking dazed and confused but unhurt.

The police and ambulance arrived, their lights flashing. They wrapped people in blankets and walked them away from the house. Aunt Corinne and I overheard Harry talking to a police officer.

"We were all dancin', havin' a good time," he said, "when all of a sudden the foundation gave way. It's a miracle we're alive. A miracle."

Was it?

Aunt Corinne and I knew the truth ... but we weren't talking.